The Horror Collection

Silver Edition

The Horror Collection: Silver Edition © 2020
Kevin J. Kennedy

Edited by Kevin J. Kennedy

Cover design by Michael Bray

First Printing, 2020

Other Books by KJK Publishing

Collections
Dark Thoughts
Vampiro and Other Strange Tales of the Macabre

Anthologies
Collected Christmas Horror Shorts
Collected Easter Horror Shorts
Collected Halloween Horror Shorts
Collected Christmas Horror Shorts 2
The Horror Collection: Gold Edition
The Horror Collection: Black Edition
The Horror Collection: Purple Edition
The Horror Collection: White Edition
100 Word Horrors
100 Word Horrors 2
100 Word Horrors 3
100 Word Horrors 4
Carnival of Horror

Novels and Novellas
Pandemonium by J.C. Michael
You Only Get One Shot by Kevin J. Kennedy & J.C. Michael
Screechers by Kevin J. Kennedy & Christina Bergling

Foreword

Although I am pulling back with the anthologies, I made the decision to continue with The Horror Collection series. These books are mini anthos and it means I can do them alongside other projects. They allow me to work with some of my favourite authors and bring their work to you on a fairly regular basis. When I discover a new author and enjoy their work, it means I can go to them and ask them to write a story for me. I don't think I could ever walk away from anthologies completely, but I do need to free up time to write more. This is book five in the series and book six is already underway. I hope you enjoy this one as much as I enjoyed putting it together.

Kevin J. Kennedy
Editor

Acknowledgements

I'd like to thank my pre readers, Darren Tarditi and Ann Keeran. I'd also like to thank everyone who picked up a copy of the book and who continue to support me, and to the authors who continue to work alongside me. A big thanks to my wife who tries her best to let me get on with all the book stuff that I do, even though it really drives her nuts.

Kevin

Table of Contents

Won't You Open the Door?
Steve Stred
Page 11

Hooch and Honey
Kevin J. Kennedy
Page 51

The Blood-Soaked Branches of the Bullingdon
Family Tree
Lex H. Jones
Page 77

Death, She Said
Edward Lee
Page 121

Forbidden Fruit
Calvin Demmer
Page 147

Won't You Open the Door?

By

Steve Stred

1.

"Please, won't you open the door?"

The old hag's voice woke him from his sleep. Alexander had stayed awake until the fire had burned down to just coals, but when her wretched voice made its way through the door of the cabin he'd bolted upright, hand finding his rifle automatically.

He cursed the floorboards as they creaked. He wanted to make it to the window nearest the door and look out, confirm he wasn't just hearing things, that she'd come and was outside.

"Won't you please let me in? It's awfully cold and I heard the howl of a wolf."

Her voice had softened but he wasn't so foolish to believe the hag had been replaced by a young lady seeking refuge.

As he neared the door he crouched down to peer underneath. His heart wished that no feet would be visible and to his surprise there weren't any.

This made him stop and think. Maybe he *was* imagining the voice?

He shuffled over to the window, keeping his body low, not wanting to be seen.

He took a breath and gripped his rifle, *too tight,* he thought, letting his hands relax. Father had told him to have soft hands when firing the gun. *"If you're rigid, boy, your aim won't be true."*

He squeezed his eyes shut, then steeled himself to look outside. The night was clear and the moon provided enough light to allow him to view the porch before the door.

Nothing.

No old crone, no young beauty.

Ah, hell. It had been my mind playing tricks on me, he thought.

He turned to walk back to his bed. Maybe he'd get the fire up and going again, take the chill off. A noise from the window stole his attention back.

Looking, he saw a decayed finger tapping on the glass. The nail had to be two inches in length and as he watched it tap, it began to move in a circular motion. Before he could figure out what was happening the glass fell inward, a perfect circle cut open in its place.

"Won't you open the door, dear?"

He stood, the tapping noise ringing in his ears. He could feel his legs moving, carrying him across the short space between the fireplace and the door. He wanted to yell out and stop himself but he couldn't, the tapping he'd heard holding him in a trance-like stupor.

His hand reached out and he felt the knob turn in his hand, the door unlatch and begin to swing inwards as he pulled it open.

On the porch – the hag.

She was a small lady, maybe five feet at most, but she was hovering two feet off the ground below. She smiled at him, exposing her decayed gums. She had no teeth so when she chuckled her festering tongue lolled around freely.

"You?"

"Such a good boy," she said before lunging at him.

It was over in moments. She feasted on his neck, drinking deep of his blood.

She left his corpse on the floor, before disappearing into the woods under the cloudless black sky.

2.

His body was found several days later, when his father and brother came searching. They had planned on coming to visit Alexander, so when they arrived they were shaken.

"It was a witch, Father. I have no doubt," young Ezekiel said as they examined the corpse of his sibling. The body had been drained of all of its blood, and while a few critters had come and had a few bits and bites from his flesh, he was otherwise untouched.

"We must bury your brother. Then, we will avenge him."

They each took an end, carrying the body outside. Without life and without blood, they were surprised with how light he was.

Retrieving two shovels, they began to dig.

By midday sweat shone on their foreheads, frequent sleeve wiping was needed to keep their eyes from stinging.

"Father, we could see if brother has any water or food."

Ezekiel used his shovel as a prop, leaning into it while supporting his weight with his arms.

"We will not enter into that cursed place again," the old man replied. "Why look," he pointed to the trees nearby, "even now the trees near this grave have started to turn."

Sure enough, Ezekiel saw the base of each trunk turning black. As he looked closer he spotted movement. Kneeling now to inspect it, he leaned in before suddenly leaping backwards. Dozens of snakes were now birthing from the bark of the tree. The hissing rose in volume as more and more wiggling reptiles pushed forth and fell into a ball on the ground at the base of the tree.

"Back up, boy. This is the work of the devil," Father said. The two retreated from the hole they'd been digging. They watched as the writhing mass made its way to the body, before consuming it and then dropping over the edge of the grave.

"Do we fill it in with dirt, Father?"

"No. We leave. We leave and we never come back to these miserable grounds again."

They untied their horses, pulling themselves onto the saddles. They took a moment to watch the open grave, ensuring that nothing crawled from it, then Ezekiel waited as his father set fire to the cabin.

The heat of the flames faded quickly as they rode towards home.

3.

Ezekiel dreamed of the snakes for weeks after, but soon the incident was forgotten. He missed his brother greatly, but due to the circumstances surrounding his passing, his parents forbid his name from being brought up around the dinner table.

It wasn't until a decade later, when his father passed away, that things from the past made themselves known again.

4.

They decided to follow the family traditions for burying Mr. Thomas. Ezekiel brought the horse and cart to the mortuary. They loaded his dead father's body into a wooden coffin, then slid it onto the deck of the cart. Ezekiel drove the cart down Main Street, clanging the funeral bell every ten seconds. As the cart travelled, mourners fell in behind, walking along until they reached the cemetery.

While the graveyard workers delicately lowered the casket into the grave, Ezekiel felt his chest tighten. He felt his arms clenching, the nails puncturing the flesh of his palms. He could feel the blood seep out and collect between his fingers before finally it dripped to the ground below. He watched as the sun dimmed and the clouds darkened.

As the priest delivered the eulogy and quoted some bible passages, Ezekiel could swear he saw movement from the walls of the grave. It hit him then – *the trees*. He remembered how snakes had come forth from the trunks of the trees when they'd been digging his brother's grave.

Now, he watched as the dirt started to crumble and oblong shapes started to push their way out of the soil. The workers now noticed what was happening and scrambled out of the hole.

While the rest of the gathered mourners screamed and fled in horror, Ezekiel walked to the edge of his father's grave and watched with shock as hundreds and then thousands of snakes filled the opening.

When they finally broke the ridge and started to slither away, Ezekiel left.

Something had cursed his brother and was passed to his father. Now, as the last living male in the Thomas family, it would pass to him. He decided then, that he would have to return to that damned land.

5.

Ezekiel drank himself stupid for a week after his father was buried. He drank to forget, and he drank to build up some liquid courage. Whatever was causing this series of events was such that it was making him question his bravery.

He'd asked a few of his friends to aid him, giving them the barest of details. Only his childhood friend, Oliver had agreed to come along. This warmed his heart. Oliver was the most pragmatic person Ezekiel had ever met. This would do them well if anything peculiar was to occur.

Once his headache left and he stopped spilling his guts, he called on Oliver and the two saddled up their horses and turned towards Ezekiel's brother's land.

6.

On the second day of their trip, Oliver began to notice owls. They were flying through the trees, swooping through the sky or simply sitting on branches watching the duo.

"That's not normal behaviour," Oliver mentioned, a shiver running through Ezekiel.

They stopped on the bank of the river to set up camp. They tied the horses up and made a fire, then fashioned a lean-to with some downed branches and a thick blanket.

Ezekiel tossed and turned, the eyes of the owls peppering his dreams.

7.

In the morning, Oliver found that the horses had broken free during the night. Ezekiel questioned that, saying that it looked like the reins had been cut through as he inspected what was left behind.

Either way, that meant they had to make their way on foot now. Oliver chatted about how strange the growth patterns looked of the surrounding forest, while Ezekiel ignored his friend and tried to determine just what his brother had stumbled on.

He thought back to the day when he and his father had found his brother. He hated saying his name, even thinking it was tough, but Alexander had been a great older brother to him and his death still caused him grief.

8.

On the fourth night while the two ate a light dinner and reminisced about their childhood, a scream intruded into the stillness of the surrounding forest.

Both men bolted to their feet, looking in all directions.

"What the hell was that?" Oliver asked, his face as white as a sheet.

"Damned if I know," Ezekiel replied. They circled the edge of the campfire light, trying to see if someone was near. With no luck they returned to the warmth by the flames.

"I ain't going to be sleeping tonight," Oliver tried to joke, but Ezekiel didn't laugh in reply. Instead he was fixated on the path they'd arrived on.

"Someone just ran across that trail, up there," he said, pointing down the way.

"You sure?"

"Yup," he replied. He sat and stared for what felt like an eternity, watching to see if the figure darted across again.

His eyes finally betrayed him and sleep took over. Oliver followed soon behind.

As the two men's heads dropped to their chest and soft snores started, a sickly figure stood in the pathway. It lurched forward, towards the duo, feet scuffing the ground, entrails dragging behind it.

When it made it to the edge of the light it stopped and let out another god-awful scream.

Ezekiel and Oliver woke with a start, finding that whatever had made the noise had disappeared into the forest.

9.

"Ok, level with me," Oliver said the next morning as they approached the edge of Ezekiel's brother's land. "What's really going on here?"

"Some*thing* killed my brother and my father. I think whatever it was has cursed my family. It passed between them. Now, I need to stop it, before it stops me."

Oliver stood expressionless. Ezekiel could see the wheels turning as he processed the information.

"Right."

"I swear on my life. Did you not see what happened at my father's funeral?" he asked. He knew Oliver had personally witnessed the arrival of the snakes.

"That same thing happened when we were burying Alexander. Snakes began to birth from the surrounding trees. It got to the point that me and father torched my brother's cabin and fled."

Oliver solemnly nodded, unease growing throughout his body.

After a few more paces Ezekiel realized that he was walking alone. He turned to find Oliver standing on the roadway. When Ezekiel approached he found his friend was shaking, eyes wet with tears ready to flee down his cheeks.

"Oliver, are you ok?"

"I'm afraid I've pissed myself," he replied.

Ezekiel put a hand on his shoulder, squeezing the man firmly.

"If you need to return home, I won't judge you any less. I would appreciate the help and your companionship. Truth be told, I've never been this afraid in my life. I would understand if you departed."

Oliver shook his head.

"No. A friend needs me. You've been my dearest friend since as long as I can remember. You'd never abandon me. I apologize for my current state, but I will continue."

They shook hands and carried on.

After some time, Ezekiel decided to ask Oliver some pointed questions.

"Oliver. Do you believe in the devil?"

"I can't say I do, Ezekiel. While I am a firm believer in God and the word of the bible, I don't believe that there is a single figure out there, waiting to capture wayward souls."

Ezekiel took in what his friend had said, then asked his next question.

"What about demons and witches?"

As he asked the question a dozen ravens cawed before swooping down at the duo. They ducked and rolled on the dirt, trying to stay out of range from their talons.

"Run!" Ezekiel said as the birds regrouped, turning to swarm the men.

Oliver took off at a dead sprint, his leather shoes slapping hard against the ground. Ezekiel did his best to keep up, but the birds were faster.

He felt their sharp beaks start hitting his exposed neck, causing him to somersault and then tumble out of control. When he finally stopped, he looked around, finding the birds had turned their wrath onto Oliver. His friend was trying to bat them away with a branch he'd found, swinging at the ravens as they dive-bombed him over and over.

As Ezekiel searched for another stick to help his friend, he saw one of the black bastards swoop in and viciously claw his face. His cheek opened up and blood began to spurt out.

Oliver dropped his branch and took off running again. As Ezekiel arrived where his friend had been, the ravens appeared to have lost interest, deciding to turn and fly away, leaving him standing there holding a stick.

"Oliver! They've gone," he yelled, running after him.

He caught up to him a short distance later, Oliver sitting on the side of the path. He was holding a hand to his face and Ezekiel could see blood had made its way in between his fingers.

"It hurts. It hurts and it burns," he said as Ezekiel jogged up to him.

Ezekiel inspected his wound. He found the edges to be bubbling and the skin looked burned, as though Oliver had been doused with acid. His hand was the same.

"Those ravens. Whatever they were, they weren't normal birds," Oliver said then. "To answer your question, I don't believe in demons or witches. Look at the foolishness over in Salem. But, I do believe in evil as a power. I can't fully rationalize it and say *why*, just that I firmly believe a person can harness it and do bad with it. I think this is one of those times."

Ezekiel gave Oliver his handkerchief, letting his friend use it to put pressure on his cheek. It looked like the wound was getting worse minute by minute.

"If you're still up for it, I say we try and cover more ground. We might be able to make the location where Alexander's cabin was before dark."

Oliver got up and they continued on.

Behind them, the forest closed over the pathway, making it appear as though it had never been there at all.

10.

When they arrived at the edge of his brother's property, Ezekiel paused.

"Look at the trees," he said to Oliver, pointing to the forest edge around them. Alexander had spent a half decade harvesting the land, removing growth with plans for a farm and a large garden. The trees now all had holes throughout them, from the ground to about five feet up. The two men could see through the holes, as though someone had drilled straight through with a piece of metal.

"Those are from snakes. I know it," Ezekiel meekly said, wishing those words didn't exist. All around the bases of the trees they could see where things had slithered away, the leaves pushed into thin paths.

"Wherever they went, I'm glad. It means they ain't here," Oliver quipped as he stepped forward into the opening. Ezekiel found that he couldn't take that step. That he was against an invisible barrier that was preventing him from moving ahead.

"You coming?"

Ezekiel nodded and forced his feet forward, feeling his body shiver as he crossed the property threshold.

Oliver was walking faster now, Ezekiel not sure why. When his friend arrived at the top of the short hill, he turned, his face contorted with confusion.

"I thought you said you guys burned your brother's cabin down?"

When Ezekiel arrived beside Oliver, he was dumbfounded.

There it was. The cabin. As good as new.

"I don't understand. Father torched it."

Oliver strode confidently to the building, while Ezekiel took his time.

Nothing about this scenario felt natural. Ezekiel could feel his skin crawl and the hair on his arms stand at attention, the closer he got to the house. It was as though an energy was being transmitted from the cabin, an energy that only he could feel.

Oliver appeared to not notice it. He walked directly to the front door. Looking at his friend, he knocked once and when the door opened, he stepped inside with a smile on his face. The door slammed shut behind him and a scream came from within. Ezekiel rushed forward, pounding on the door, kicking at the hinges, trying desperately to get inside. He grabbed the door knob, feeling the metal burn into his palm. He yelled in pain, but didn't pull away. He needed to get inside, needed to save his friend.

The screaming reached an ear-shattering pitch, before coming to a sudden end. Ezekiel stepped away from the door, not wanting to look inside, but drawn to the window by the door.

He noticed scratch marks on the surface of the glass. He didn't want to know what made them, instead he blocked it from his mind as he looked through.

There, sitting on a chair by the fire was Oliver.

Ezekiel tried the door, finding it opened with ease. Stepping into the cabin, he was met with the aroma of fresh baked bread and coffee.

"Ah, Ezekiel, I was wondering when you'd catch up," Oliver said.

Rubbing his eyes and smacking his face, Ezekiel looked at his friend.

"How is this possible? I heard you scream in agony? Even your face is healed." Ezekiel looked at his own palms, finding no burns on them as well.

Oliver walked to his friend and gave him a once over, concern on his face.

"Are you ok, Ezekiel? Dehydrated? What happened to my face?"

Ezekiel wasn't sure what to believe now. He sat down, feeling the exhaustion in his muscles as he let his legs splay out before him.

Oliver brought him a cup of coffee, steam coming off the liquid.

"Thank you, very kind," he said, accepting the drink.

"I'm going to prepare some dinner. Then I think we can both use a good night's sleep," his friend replied, heading to the kitchen area.

Ezekiel had two deep drinks of his coffee before the hazy arrival of slumber started to bob his head. *I should get up and help Oliver*, he thought as his eyes closed and he slumped sideways.

In the kitchen his friend's eyes glowed red and a grin spread wide on his face.

11.

Ezekiel woke up some time during the night. He found himself naked in bed, unsure of how he got there or when he got there. He looked around the darkened room and recognized it as being his brother's old room. At one time Alexander was going to expand the cabin and add a second floor, but he found it too difficult to accomplish on his own. So there was still the beginning of some stairs along the one wall, which always seemed weird to Ezekiel. Why hadn't his brother ever removed them?

He heard a rhythmic swishing noise coming from the living area. He could make out the red glow of flames from the fire pit through the open doorway. Not bothering to get dressed, he walked to the door and looked out.

The scene before him made him cover his mouth, not wanting a scream to grab unwanted attention.

Oliver was kneeling before the fire. Standing beside him was a rail-thin woman. Both were naked. Her belly was distended, hanging down over her crotch. From where he stood, Ezekiel could see movement below her skin, as though something was trying to push its way out. The swishing noise was the sound of the hag using her thickened nails to intricately slice back row upon row of Oliver's skin. She'd already stripped his right side and was now working on his left side. The skin hung from his muscles like string from a balloon.

The woman was humming as she sliced into Oliver again, dragging her nail down his back. Then she grasped the top of the strip and tugged it away as she pulled it down, draping it below.

Ezekiel felt the room grow dizzy, his knees shaking and buckling. He was going to vomit but couldn't focus on anything.

"Ah, Ezekiel. So glad you could join us," the crone spoke.

The room spun to black and Ezekiel felt his impact on the floor. His vision spun, the last thing he saw was her crusted feet walking towards him.

12.

"Breakfast is ready."

Oliver's voice brought him from his sleep.

Ezekiel swung his legs from the bed, stood and stretched.

He felt refreshed.

Joining Oliver in the kitchen, he saw some boiled potatoes on a plate with some eggs.

"Thank you," he said, taking his plate.

"How did you sleep?" Oliver asked, before taking a drink.

"I had horrible dreams. Awful dreams. Oddly, I feel refreshed. Rejuvenated. You?"

Oliver smiled, sipping some more of his drink.

"Never better," he replied, setting the cup down. "Never better."

13.

The day was spent inspecting the property. Oliver suggested they stay together, telling Ezekiel that he didn't feel comfortable on his own.

They found all of the trees to be the same – holes bored through. In the farthest corner of the property they found hundreds of shed snake skins. When Oliver stooped down and picked some up, they disintegrated, blowing away like dust.

While returning to the cabin, Ezekiel spotted something through the trees. Motioning to his friend, they stepped off the property and into the forest, wanting to inspect what had caught his eye.

There on a fallen tree were the displayed skeletons of a dozen owls and a dozen ravens.

Oliver called for his friend to come see something. Against his better judgement, Ezekiel went and when he arrived he wished he'd turned and walked to the cabin instead.

The talons of the last raven were caked in dried blood. As Oliver stood, his cheek opened up again, the flap of skin making a slapping noise as it flopped open and connected with his face.

"We need to leave," he said calmly, as though he was looking at something completely different than Ezekiel.

The two made their way back to the cabin. They stopped at the front door, sharing a panicked look. The door was open.

"You closed it, yes?" Ezekiel asked.

"Of course, we both waited while I bolted it, remember?"

Ezekiel did, which made this discovery all the more concerning.

Upon entering they saw the place was in disarray, as though a lawman had ransacked their residence, looking for contraband.

"Who did this?" Oliver asked, still paying no mind to his exposed cheek.

Ezekiel didn't have an answer. Instead they closed and barricaded the door. They spent the rest of the day returning the living quarters to some sort of order.

As the sun began to descend towards setting, Ezekiel felt dread pulse through his veins.

"Oliver. Promise me, promise me that we won't go to sleep. Promise me that the two of us will stay awake until morning. Once the sun rises, we'll run back as fast as we can. We'll get a priest and we'll let them cleanse these lands."

Oliver nodded, eyes staring vacantly ahead.

14.

It had been dark for a few hours when there was three loud knocks on the door.

The two men had remained sitting near the fire in silent thought, each keeping watch on the other.

"Please, won't you open the door?"

A voice as old as time spoke through the wood, through the barricade.

Ezekiel jumped to his feet. Oliver joined him and the two watched the door, expecting the wood to burst inward.

"Oliver? Ezekiel? Please let me in, it's so very cold." The voice that spoke was now the voice of Alexander. Oliver had to grab his friend, hold him back.

"That's not your brother," he said, firmly.

Three more forceful knocks on the door.

"Let me in you ungrateful boy," the voice of Ezekiel's father bellowed.

Oliver crept to the window beside the door. When he finally looked out, Ezekiel watched as his friend's body went rigid. He turned to Ezekiel, color drained from his face.

"She's floating," he said.

Then the window exploded, glass slicing into Oliver's head. The top of his scalp was cut open, peeling his hair back. A rotting hand entered through the jagged opening and ripped Oliver's head from his neck.

The body slumped to the floor as the head was pulled into the darkness outside.

"Oh, I'll come in. One way or another. Just you wait," the hag called out.

Ezekiel grabbed the iron fire poker and held it out before him. He shuffled forward, making his way to the body of his friend. Keeping his distance, he looked outside. The front porch was clear, the hag having fled.

He went back and sat on his chair by the fire. He vowed to stay awake, to not fall asleep. Soon, the adrenaline caught up and he began to crash. As his head bobbed and his eyes fought to stay open, he caught a glimpse of movement by the window.

Squinting, he saw Oliver's head had been impaled on a shard of broken glass. As he fell asleep, he saw his friend's detached head lick its lips.

15.

The rumbling of his stomach signalled it was time for Ezekiel to wake up. He found he was back in bed, once again having no recollection of how he made it there.

Looking out through the window in the room, he found the sun was beginning to set. He'd slept through the entire day.

Entering the living area, he found that during his sleep Oliver's body had been snatched, a trail of blood showing where it had been dragged through the broken window. Peering outside, he could follow the blood pathway all the way to the edge of the trees. There he found Oliver's body, strung up by his innards between two dying birch.

"What do you want?" Ezekiel yelled into the black.

His question was answered by three hard knocks on the door, causing him to jump back away from the window.

"All I want, is for you to open the door," the woman's voice replied.

Behind him the fire erupted, flames dancing high and wide from the hearth. Ezekiel looked in horror as the blaze caught the wood surrounding, the cabin beginning to burn.

"I lived on these lands, raised my kids here. Grew old and was happy. Then that Alexander comes along and takes what wasn't his. All I wanted was to rest in peace. Buried here in this land, *my* land, but instead your brother digs up my bones and desecrates my grave."

It all clicked then. His brother had stolen this property. Now the family was paying.

"I'm sorry. I'm so sorry. I don't know why Alexander did that," he cried, dropping to his knees.

"Your apology means nothing. If you won't open the door, then you can stay inside and burn."

Ezekiel got to his feet and rushed to the door, trying to open it. He found it was immoveable. He tried pulling it and turning it, but no amount of effort would budge it. He then went to the broken window to try and climb out but found the crone had barricaded the opening from the outside, heavy logs stacked up against the cabin.

He could hear her laughing from beyond the door.

The flames grew hotter and higher, his clothes now burning. His skin bubbled, blistered and burst.

As the yard beyond the house whistled with the arrival of thousands of snakes, a pained scream could be heard from inside the inferno.

The lady made her way to the edge of the forest, pausing to listen to Ezekiel's final sounds, before disappearing into the blackness beyond.

16.

When Ezekiel and Oliver didn't return, their friends sent out a search party. For two weeks they searched to no avail, unable to find a trace of the duo.

Making it all the more difficult was that where the path should have been, most of it was now grown over or appeared to have never existed. The group had to slash through underbrush and chop down trees to make any progress.

Finally, after making it to Alexander's former property, they found two graves. One had a small stone with the letter 'A' crudely carved into it, which they believed to be Alexander's. The other grave had a plank of wood placed on it. The name 'Lauren' was scratched into the surface.

The group said some last rites for the two, then saddled up and started the journey back to town.

When they left the edge of the property, they heard the familiar sounds of owls hooting from the forest.

They didn't see the rotting, head-less remains of Oliver's body in the trees, or the burned corpse of Ezekiel draped over a rock just off the pathway as they rode.

The End

Hooch and Honey

By

Kevin J. Kennedy

Daniel had always known he would leave home on his sixteenth birthday. He would have left sooner but his mother always guilted him into staying. When he turned sixteen though, he was a man and had to make his own way in the world. It was nineteen twenty-two and times were changing. Jazz was the music of choice and fashion had entered a new phase.

Having saved up some money from doing odd jobs around town, Daniel felt like he was well set for his adventure. He had no idea how unprepared he was for the real world.

Less than two weeks had passed before Daniel had spent his earnings. He refused to go home but had so far been unable to gain employment. One of his fondest memories of the adventure thus far was an evening spent in an underground club. He had danced and laughed and more importantly, drunk alcohol. It was his first time but the young lady that had latched onto his arm had insisted. It had burned as he had swallowed it, but shortly afterward, he felt a warm glow in his stomach that spread throughout his body. He felt a little lightheaded but in a good way. They had danced for hours afterward, every so often stopping to have another drink. That's where most of his money had gone.

Sitting in a cold doorway, watching the world pass by, Daniel decided that this was the place he would find employment. It was busy and money seemed to flow into the place. Whil there he had noticed that the club owners were dressed better than everyone else and were given a high level of respect from everyone. That was the kind of life Daniel had always seen himself living.

He made his way back to the club, but it hadn't opened yet. He thought he would need to come back later when the door sprung open.

"Hey kid, what you doing?" came a gruff voice from the darkened doorway.

"Uh... I was... I'm looking to speak to the owner. I need a job." Daniel stuttered.

A laugh came from the figure.

"Come inside kid."

Daniel, feeling nervous, made his way down the stairs to the club and followed the dark figure inside. The club was empty but noises floated in from the back room.

The man who had let him in, nodded to follow him and they made their way through the tables to the doorway at the back of the club. He held it open but didn't enter. Daniel felt nervous but knew that if he turned and fled, he would still be without work and would face being a homeless bum or face the even worse fate, of having to return home with his tail between his legs. He kept moving until he was in the doorway. The large man stood holding it open for him.

When Daniel walked inside, he quickly scanned the room. There were four men sitting playing cards in the centre of the room. There was a glass bottle filled with what looked like the alcohol he had previously tried, glasses in front of each of the men and several ashtrays with cigarettes or cigars. The room was in a cloud of smoke. As he took the rest in, he noticed that the room contained only the table and several barrels. He guessed they were filled with alcohol. He looked at the men, unsure of what to say when one of them spoke.

"What you want kid?" It was another large figure who had a cigar clamped between his teeth. Daniel recognised him from the night he had been here dancing. He was one of the men that some treated with respect and others gave a wide berth.

"I'm looking for work." Was all he could think to reply.

"Work... Everybody works kid. Only some get paid."

The other men around the table laughed at this.

Daniel wasn't quite sure what was so funny. He wondered who would work without pay. He didn't know what else to do or say, so he just stood there feeling small and stupid.

"You looking to get paid kid?"

Daniel knew he wanted to get paid but wondered if it was a trick question.

"Yeah, I left home and had some money, but I've spent it. I need to make some more. I don't want to have to go back home."

All four men turned and looked at Daniel now, making him feel even smaller. Everything was silent for a moment and then they burst out laughing.

"I like this kid," one of them said.

"Boy doesn't want to go home," another said.

Again, Daniel wasn't sure what was so funny.

"Come over here." The large man who had spoke to him first said.

Daniel walked over to the table and stood between him and another of the men.

"You know what we do here son?" Daniel was asked. He guessed that the large man was the leader.

"Yeh, it's a dancing club and you sell hooch."

The men burst into laughter again.

"No flies on this lad," one of them said.

"And who told you that lado?"

"No one. I was here a few nights ago. I had some and I danced with one of the girls."

A large smile broke out across the leader's face. "You know, I think I like him too," he said to the other men.

"Go and pull that spare chair over son," he told Daniel.

Daniel walked over to the only spare chair in the room and pulled it into a space two of the men made for him. He sat up on it and leant his arms on the table. He noticed that there was a lot of money in the pot and wondered if he would ever have that kind of money.

"So, you want to sell hooch, boy?"

"I want to get paid." Daniel said, thinking it was the right answer and knowing it was true.

The men laughed again. Daniel had never felt so funny in all his life.

"A man after my own heart," the man in the black fedora said. He wore a white shirt opened to the chest.

"Don't we all," said another, wearing a pinstriped blue fedora. He was much slighter in build than the other three but by far the most terrifying. From either side of his mouth, deep red scars, drew back to his ears, giving him the appearance of an evil clown without any makeup on.

Noticing Daniel looking at the scars, the leader decided to introduce the men.

"That there is Chelsea. Pretty, ain't he. Those there scars are called a Chelsea smile and he's had them since he was a boy younger than yourself."

Daniel looked back to Chelsea. He smiled wide, making himself look even more terrifying.

"Man, who was sewing my old mum gave me these. Fourteen I was. He said I had a big mouth one time I spoke back to him and gave me these with a bread knife."

Daniels mouth hung open in shock.

"S'okay though. That night I buried that knife in his heart. Won't be scarring up any more innocent children. I had to go on the run of course but that's how I met up with these fine fellows. Reckon my life turned out pretty good, all things considered." Finishing his statement, he picked up his glass, downed the hooch and poured another. While doing so, he topped up the other glasses and filled one for Daniel, sitting it in front of him.

"I haven't got any money," Daniel said.

"Don't worry about that kiddo. We don't pay for the drink. We make it, then we get paid. He smiled again. It was no less frightening now that Daniel knew the back story.

The leader continued introducing them. "The handsome fella that never takes off the black fedora

59

is Lefty, the large fellow on your right is Brick and I'm Lansky. We run this side of town and this club is the coolest spot around."

"Don't the police ever try and shut you down?" Daniel asked, wondering how they get away with it all.

The men all laughed again.

Lefty spoke this time. "We pay them off, kid. I drop money to a few of them each month and they stay away. Well, I say they stay away. Most of them come here to have a drink after their shift finishes. Hell, we even have judges who come here for a drink. Most of them would have nowhere to go but home to their wives if this place shut down. We just pay them to make sure they keep the do-gooders in line. There's always one who wants to spoil the party for everyone else, but they are always taken care of by the guys on the payroll."

Daniel sat back for a minute, trying to take everything he had been told in.

"So, what do I have to do?" He asked them.

"There's always stuff needing done. You can help Lefty make the drops, help make the hooch, sometimes we need to deal with others that are trying to move onto our turf. You can help us with that. There's never a shortage of work, but like we said, we get paid."

A little worried about what dealing with others who moved onto their turf meant, Daniel decided it wasn't worth thinking about too much. The men seemed to be confident and have everything under control and looking at the jewellery they wore, coupled with the stacks of money on the table was proof enough that they did in fact *get paid.*

Daniel bit his lip for a while, trying to work up the courage to ask his next question. Lansky noticed and asked him, "What's on your mind kid?"

"I was wondering… I don't have any money right now. Could I maybe get an advance and work to pay it off?"

At this the table erupted into hysterical laughter.

"You've got balls kid. I like it." Lansky told him. "Why do you need the money so quickly?"

"I don't have anywhere to stay. I need money to get a room," Daniel replied, looking down.

"Nonsense. You stay with us now."

Daniel smiled. This was the first friends he had made since leaving home. Well, he had met the girl, but he hadn't seen her since. He hoped he would meet her again in the bar one night. He reached across the table and picked up his drink and downed it. The men smiled at him. Chelsea picked up a few notes from the bundle in front of him and sat them next to Daniel's hand.

"That'll start you off kid. Was all he said.

The rest of the evening was spent drinking and smoking. Daniel had never even tried smoking before but by the end of the night, he was getting the hang of it. He couldn't keep up with his new friends with the hooch though. A few times he felt dizzy and thought he would fall off of his chair. A few hours later the club was ready to open, and Lansky took him upstairs and showed him a spare room above the club.

"This is your room now kid. It's pretty bare but you will be earning so you can buy what you want to put in it. For now, it'll give you somewhere to bring the girls. I'll take you tomorrow and get you some nice clothes and then we will show you the ropes."

Lansky left the room and seconds later Daniel was asleep on his new bed. He wasn't used to the hooch yet and it had been a full day of new experiences.

When Daniel awoke the following morning, he felt like someone had been beating him around the head. Opening his eyes seemed like a giant feat. It took him a while but eventually he got up and got dressed. He wandered downstairs to the once again empty club. He had woken a few times through the night and heard the club in full swing, but he still felt too dizzy and fell straight back asleep.

He knocked on the door to the room where he had spent most of yesterday.

"Come in." He heard called through the door.

He opened the door and entered. Lansky, Brick, Chelsea and Lefty all sat round the table but this time there was no hooch, cards or money.

"Hey kid. You don't look so good," Lefty said.

"I'll be okay. Just not used to the hooch," he told them.

They each smiled but no one laughed at him this time.

"Well, I hope you aren't too under the weather. We need to show you how things work around here," Lansky said.

"I'm okay. Got to earn my keep," Daniel replied.

Lansky clapped his hands, stood up, and said "good, let's get moving then." He stepped around the table, walked over to Daniel, put his hand on his shoulder and led him back out of the room. They walked over behind the bar and Lansky filled two shot glasses.

"Drink this kid. It'll have you feeling better in no time."

Daniel really didn't want another drink, but he also didn't want to appear weak. He lifted the glass and knocked back the shot. He almost vomited straight away. He could feel his mouth filling with saliva. He kept swallowing it back down, trying his best not to let it show on his face, but his eyes were watering. It eventually passed. When it did, he looked back at Lansky. He had been watching him the whole time.

"You did good kid. Now, let's get moving."

Lansky only walked a few steps then leaned down and pulled a rug aside. Under it was a square wooden trap door. He pulled on the brass metal ring handle and it creaked open. Without saying anything, Lansky began to climb down the ladder.

Daniel could already feel the booze working its magic. While the warmth in his stomach left him unsure if he may vomit at some point, it was beginning to settle, but he didn't feel half as bad as he had before the drink. The pain in his head was easing and he no longer felt the need to go straight back to bed. When Lansky was out of sight, Daniel begun his descent down the ladder too.

When Daniel arrived at the bottom of the ladder, Lansky was waiting on him by a large wooden door. The room they were in looked like an old dungeon. The walls were rough stone, it stunk of dampness and it was completely empty apart from the ladder.

"Now kid, what you are about to see is how we run our business. You wanted in so you need to be able to deal with everything. You ready?"

While Daniel had no idea what he was just about to see, he knew there was only one answer to the question. He wanted to make some money, but he also knew at this point if he changed his mind that he might just disappear. He was under no illusion that the men he now worked for didn't just invite people down here and then let them walk straight back out the door.

"I'm ready," Daniel said, trying to sound confident. He seen Lansky smile.

"Good lad." With the statement, Lansky pulled open the door.

As much as Daniel had been trying to prepare himself for anything, he could have never prepared for what was in front of him.

"Come on in kid," Lansky said, entering the room.

Daniel followed but couldn't keep his head still. He didn't know where to look. The room was filled with naked men and women. A lot of them were emaciated. Each moved slowly performing various tasks. This would have been enough to give Daniel nightmares for quite some time, but the real horror in the room lay against the back wall. Almost the entire wall was hidden behind what appeared to be a humongous white grub. It was lying on its side and it almost touched the roof of the dungeon like room.

Wall to wall must have been near twenty foot and it reached both ends. It shone a little, even in the candle light and its skin looked waxy. Along it's body, every two or three feet, taps had been screwed into its skin. The naked people were carrying bottles over to it and turning the taps on, filling the bottles and then stacking them across the room.

The whole time, Lansky just stood watching Daniel for his reaction. He wasn't sure if the kid would run out of the room, throw up or pass out. So far, he had done none of them. Enough time passed and he was still standing taking it all in.

"This is how we make our hooch kid." He informed him, knowing that Daniel had probably worked that out for himself but hoping to get some sort of response from him.

"But… But… You guys drink this?" was the only thing Daniel could think to say.

"Course we do kid. Best hooch in the state. It's free and we don't need to run it across state lines."

"Does anyone know apart from you guys?"

"Just the crew kid, and that's how it'll stay. You're one of us now and one of your jobs will be bringing the hooch upstairs and putting it into barrels in the back room. You had to see how we do things. You okay with it?"

Daniel thought for a minute. "Who are the people?"

"A mixture of people who couldn't pay their debts, worked for our competitors or ran to the police about something. People who had to disappear and we felt it was better to put them to work rather than just bump them off." Lansky paused for a minute. "Come on, let's go back upstairs," and with that he turned and climbed the ladder. Daniel followed.

The guy who had let Daniel into the club the day before, had been down in the room with them all. Daniel reasoned that he kept them working.

Lansky went on as they climbed back into the bar. "We keep them alive, but they don't get much food and they don't get any respite. They work and they sleep but they are still alive. Most hope to get out of here one day if they behave and do what they are told, but none of them are ever leaving. It's all profit for us kid and no outgoings." As he finished speaking, Lansky took his trilby off and set it on the bar before pouring two more drinks for them into the glasses they had used before going into the trap door. He knocked his back and eyed Daniel while he waited to see what his response is.

Daniel thought about it for a bit. "It's still kinda hard to believe you drink it when you have seen where it comes from. Where did you even find that thing and what is it?"

Lansky chuckled and poured himself another drink. He walked around the front of the bar and sat on one of the bar stools. He straightened his waistcoat, lit a cigarette and grabbed his drink.

"Well, it goes back a while, but we had a beef with another crew. Done some business with them and they stiffed us. We came in hot and shot the place up and took over. Seemed like a nice little club to run. We were here a few days before we found the trap door but when we did, it was already set up. They didn't have bodies down there doing the work though. They had been collecting the alcohol themselves. We just streamlined the process, and here we are."

Daniel again thought about what he was being told. It seemed completely disgusting and unethical. He had never been a bad person and he didn't want to start now. On the other hand, he had seen how well off the guys who owned the club were and he wanted a part of it.

Lansky lifted the bottle and poured himself another. "You're awful quiet, kid. Having second thoughts?"

Daniel looked back at Lansky. He lifted the shot glass and downed it. "When are you taking me for those new clothes?"

Lansky burst out laughing. "My man. Why don't we go and get you sorted out now?"

***

That evening, Daniel was back in the club. He wore the finest Italian three-piece suit and an exquisite French shirt. He had his first ever hat. He had opted for a fedora and his new leather shoes fitted him like a glove. He watched the crowd drink, dance and be merry. He was on the other side now. As he watched, he thought about the money that flowed into the till. He didn't know what his cut would be, but he had never worn clothes so impressive. He had a pocket full of cash and no worries for the first time since leaving home. He knew he was going to be asked to do some questionable things over the coming weeks and months. He also didn't know if he would live to an old age. Another crew may come along and take over, just as his crew had. It didn't matter. He could live slow and have a long hard life or he could live fast and probably die young. It was no contest. He wanted to have fun.

A few hours passed and several girls and women had approached Daniel and tried to latch onto him. Money spoke. He had rejected them all. Just after midnight, she walked in the door. The girl who had introduced him to alcohol on his first night here. He smiled and wondered if she would recognise him now. He knew she liked him before he had anything. She didn't look like she had much herself, but he knew he could trust her. He needed a good woman and if she would have him, he would show her a world she had never known. Tomorrow, they would go shopping and he would treat her to the prettiest clothes she had ever seen, and he would make sure her purse was full. What would be the point in making lots of money if he didn't have someone special to spend it with?

Daniel made his way across the bar to meet her. He stopped in front of her and she looked him up and down. "Well, don't you scrub up nice?" she said.

"What's your name?" he asked.

"Honey."

"Perfect. Let's get a drink."

He took her hand and led her to the bar where they spoke long into the night.

The End

The Blood-Soaked Branches of the Bullingdon Family Tree

By

Lex H. Jones

"That tree is dead, Mr Bullingdon." Jenna Reid remarked, staring up at the ancient oak tree before her.

"I know it may look that way, but I assure you it is not." The older man at her side replied, his hands clasped together as if in prayer. "The old girl just needs some attention, that's all. A few dead branches removed, that kind of thing."

"All the branches look dead." Jenna replied, squinting as she looked up at the tree, its gnarled and twisted limbs a dry grey colour.

"On closer inspection I'm sure you'll see otherwise. Take as long as you need, I assure you that money is no object."

"No, I imagine not." Jenna said beneath her breath, glancing back over her shoulder at the mansion estate to which she'd come. "I just need to get some things from my van, and I'll start making my preliminary plan."

"As you will." The man nodded, before clasping his hands behind his back and returning to the mansion house across the expansive lawn.

"Still pretty sure that you're dead." Jenna said to herself, tracing her fingertips down the old bark and watching as bits flaked away at her touch. Dusting her hands off, Jenna returned to her green-painted van, her company logo emblazoned on the side — a smiling tree with a branch giving a thumbs up — and grabbed her rucksack.

***

"A tree surgeon?" asked the wizened, crooked old man who sat beneath a blanket on the rocking chair.

"That's right. They prune the tree, get rid of all the dead branches." The younger Mr Bullingdon replied as he stood by the unlit fireplace.

"Whatever for?"

"It keeps the tree healthier."

"She's not going near the roots, is she?"

"Just the branches, uncle."

"Not wise for a young woman to be poking around near those roots."

"She won't be."

The living room door opened, and Jenna walked in with her green rucksack slung over her shoulder. She smiled at Mr Bullingdon, and then gave a little wave at the older man sat in the chair.

"Hello there, my name's Jenna."

"Lincoln." He replied. "Here to look at the tree, are you?"

"That's right. I'm going to try and help it along for you."

"Just be careful around those roots. Lots of rabbit warrens around here. Don't want you getting your foot stuck."

"I'll be careful, but thanks for warning me."

"Please have a seat, Miss Reid. Can I get you anything?"

"Tea would be lovely. Just whilst I sort the paperwork for you."

"Tea it is." Mr Bullingdon smiled, then marched off in what Jenna assumed was the direction of the kitchen.

"Surprised he's getting the tea himself, I assumed you'd have a butler." Jenna said to the older man with a smile.

"Can't keep them." He grunted. "Family only here. Just me, and my nephew Charles there. And his brother, but we don't see him all that much."

"No women to keep you boys in line?" Jenna asked.

"The women in our family have a way of dying in child birth. Probably a genetic thing." Lincoln said with a slow nod.

"Oh, I'm sorry. I didn't mean to offend."

"You didn't my dear." He replied with a haggard, tired old smile.

Jenna started to take some paperwork from her bag but stopped suddenly when her hands brushed against a thin white envelope. It had a blue logo on the top right, the NHS. The envelope had already been opened, and not carefully. Jenna swallowed a lump in her throat and took her hand away from the envelope, not even wanting to touch it, and then fastened her bag with the zip.

"Right then, boring paperwork time!" She enthused as Charles returned with a tray of tea. Pot, china cups, milk jug and sugar tin.

"You needn't worry about itemising the bill, whatever you need to charge will be fine." Charles insisted as he sat next to Jenna on the couch.

"You're not afraid I'll try and swindle you?" she teased.

"You have an honest face." Charles replied with a thin, barely-there smile.

"And a pretty one." Lincoln added from the corner of the room. He was old, barely able to move, but not dead.

"Well thank you very much." Jenna replied, then clicked the end of her pen and pointed to a few things on the contract. "This just tells you what you're liable for, what the work is likely to entail, and confirms you're aware the final cost may differ if the job proves more complex than initially estimated."

"That's all fine." Charles replied, taking the pen and signing the paperwork immediately. Jenna wished she had more clients like this. Usually they argued over every penny.

"Right then, I'll get my tools and ladders and start straight away." Jenna offered her hand as she rose, and Charles shook it lightly.

"Thank you, we do appreciate it."

Jenna left the room and Charles watched through the large bay window, as she walked back across the lawns to her van that was parked on the drive.

"She's a firm young one." Lincoln called over from his chair.

"Yes, thank you uncle."

"No wedding ring."

"That doesn't mean anything these days."

"Grandfather will have noticed her too. You know he's been in the mood of late."

"She's here to do a job, she isn't some addict we dragged off the street."

"Exactly. The last few were dirty, horrid. They didn't survive. But she's young, healthy, pretty. He'll notice soon if he hasn't already."

"She was sent by a company, they'd be aware of her absence."

"I know that, which is why I told her to watch out near the roots. But he won't care. He doesn't understand how the world works nowadays. He just knows what appetites he has. Spreading his wild oats. He wants a fresh line, you know that."

"We'll have to keep an eye on her then."

***

Jenna secured herself high up the tree using the harness and belt around her waist, her feet high on a strong ladder. Now that she was closer to the bark, she was surprised to find that she actually agreed with Charles; the tree wasn't dead at all. It looked grey and dry and old, but there was life in it. Sap on its bark, the odd leaf on the thin branches. How it was living on in this state remained a mystery to her, but Jenna didn't focus on it too much. Nature was always tougher than you thought it was, enduring despite all the odds set against it.

The branches fell away easily with the clippers she used, but Jenna was finding it difficult to decide which ones to leave and which to cull. Normally it was simple enough to determine which were dead and which weren't, but this wasn't quite so easy. All the branches could be dead, or they could all be alive. Still, she pressed on and used whatever judgement she could to decide which dry wood got to stay where it was and which didn't. The largest branch she'd felled so far dropped away, but rather than the usual dry crack, she heard a noise that sounded like a low groan. Jenna looked at the trunk of the tree and saw that where the branch had fallen away was a hole, about the size of her fist. Her eye fixed on the blackness within the hole, and she found herself leaning towards it. She got closer still, and then something looked back at her.

Jenna screamed out and fell back, her foot slipping on the ladder. Her harness went tight around her waist as it caught her weight, but something cracked in her side. She cried out in pain, and desperately tried to get her feet back onto the ladder. In her pain and panic, she realised that her face was now pressed against the tree, close to the hole in which she'd seen herself being watched. Something moved inside the hole, something a sickly white colour. It pulsed and bulged, then somehow opened to reveal a deep yellow eye. Jenna screamed again and felt herself black out.

**

"Miss Reid, are you alright?" Charles asked, mopping Jenna's brow with a damp cloth.

She opened her eyes and realised she was back in the living room of the mansion.

"You fainted, I found you dangling at the top of that ladder and carried you down."

"Thank you." Jenna smiled, blushing a little. She wasn't sure how the svelte man could have carried her down the ladder alone but assumed he must be stronger than he looked.

"What happened up there?"

"I thought I saw something. Inside the tree." Jenna grimaced and rubbed her forehead.

"Here, take this." Charles handed her a glass of fizzy water. "Just aspirin, the soluble kind. Works a bit faster, I find."

"Thank you. I'm a bit embarrassed really. I thought I saw...well...an eye."

"An eye?" Charles laughed. "Inside the tree?"

"In my defence I had just banged my head." Jenna smiled. She felt like she'd seen something before then too, but told herself she was mis-remembering. As she tried to sit up a sharp pain struck her side and she gasped.

"Yes, I think you've cracked a rib there." Charles sighed. "I've called an ambulance for you, but God knows how long they'll be to get out here."

"Thank you. I'm so sorry about this."

"Not at all, I'm just relieved you're alright. Now you just lay on that couch and stay comfortable, I'm going to make a pot of tea."

Charles left Jenna on the couch, Lincoln asleep beneath his blanket on the rocking chair, and made his way into the kitchen. He filled the black kettle and placed it on the stove, then turned and saw a strange figure staring at him. The figure was hunched over, face and head covered by a black cloak that was wrapped around itself.

"Jesus, Hugo!" Charles rasped, keeping his voice quiet but evidently angry. "Do you have to do that?"

"Would you prefer me to come through the front door, brother?" asked the hooded figure.

"No, fine, just don't sneak up on me like that."

"You have a guest." Hugo said sternly, his voice rasping and every breath sounding pained and full of fluid.

"Yes, I know. She will be leaving soon, she's injured."

"She won't be leaving."

"What do you mean?"

"Grandfather has seen her. And now he wants her."

"No. She's not like the others, Hugo. She'll be missed."

"He wants her." He repeated.

"Well you'll just have to tell him no. There's an ambulance coming as we speak."

"It'll never get here. The river may flood, some trees may fall. Grandfather has his ways."

"Dammit, Hugo!" Charles stepped closer to the hooded figure. "There'll be consequences if he does this!"

"There'll be some if he doesn't, brother." Hugo rasped, extending a sickly white, bulbous and deformed hand out of the robe and tapping his brother on the chest. "He wants to start a new line. And he's getting impatient. Don't think he won't wipe the slate clean if he gets angry enough."

"How would that help him? Who'd bring him new ones then, him? Is he going to get up and go out hunting?" Charles scoffed, batting the hand away from himself.

"Logic doesn't come into it. He's hungry. Starved. That takes precedence when he gets like this, and you know it does."

"What do you need me to do?" Charles sighed.

"Keep her here until he's ready. Then bring her to meet him."

"Alright. Now get out. I don't like seeing you in here."

"Don't like being reminded of your heritage, brother?" Hugo chuckled, rasping and coughing as he extended his fleshy, damp hand to stroke Charles' face.

Charles grimaced and Hugo went back to the corner of the kitchen, opening the secret panel that lay there and slipping back into the tunnel beyond. The door closed behind him and Charles failed to suppress a shudder.

***

"There we are." Charles announced, placing a tray of tea on the low table next to the couch. There was a pot and two cups on saucers, all old but in perfect condition.

"Thank you, that's really nice of you." Jenna struggled to sit up, and Charles immediately went to help her.

"Careful, don't move too quickly."

"The rain's really started to come down. I wasn't expecting a storm." Jenna noted, glancing out of the large bay windows at the deluge that had now darkened the sky.

"Nor was I." Charles said with concern, remembering what his brother had said about how easily an ambulance might be diverted. "That must be what's keeping the ambulance. If the river along the road has flooded then they'll have no way of getting here. I could try and drive you, but...

"No, don't do that. We'll be in more danger doing that than if we wait it out." Jenna suggested, as Charles knew she would.

"In that case you'll have to stay the night. We have more than enough rooms, and everything you need. I'll grab you some painkillers to take with your tea, and do everything I can to make you comfortable."

"How are you not married?" Jenna teased.

"Well, folk of my persuasion haven't been able to marry all that long." Charles replied.

"Ah, I should have seen that. Not that it's obvious, I just mean that the kind ones are always married or gay."

"I'll take that as a compliment. Would that my family saw it quite so positively."

"They're a bit old fashioned?"

"Grandfather isn't particularly fond of the idea, no. He gets rather angry at me for not providing him with offspring."

"Offspring??"

"His word, not mine." Charles chuckled. "I suppose I could adopt, but that wouldn't satisfy him. He wants children of his blood."

"Does he live here? I haven't seen anyone else besides you and Lincoln." Asked Jenna as she carefully took the tea that Charles handed to her.

"He's around, you won't see much of him though. What about yourself, anyway, since we're getting personal?"

"Erm no, I'm not married or anything. I had a boyfriend, he wanted children but, um…. It didn't work out. I still do want them, but he wasn't willing to wait anymore, and…" Jenna wiped a tear from her eye.

"Oh I'm sorry, I'm being awfully rude." Charles put a hand on Jenna's and held it gently. "We shouldn't be discussing this, it's not my business."

"Well, I started it."

"And I'm ending it before I feel like a complete arse for upsetting a guest in my care." He patted her hand and then rose. "I'll fetch you some painkillers and then make up a guest room for you, so you can retire whenever you wish."

Charles brought Jenna the tablets and then ventured up the large staircase in the hallway, leaving Jenna alone in the room. Somewhere in the adjoining room she could hear the faint sound of Lincoln snoring, but besides that the house was quiet. She held her tea tightly in her hands, fighting off the slight chill that had taken to the air. Her side hurt, but not like it had. Whatever tablets Charles had brought her worked well, and fast. She actually felt tired now, her eyes growing heavy. She was comfortable enough that she carefully leaned back on the couch, bringing her legs up to rest on the leather footstool, and closed her eyes.

"Beautiful specimen."

Jenna's eyes opened immediately, and she scanned the room. Nothing. There was nobody there. No source for the voice. Lincoln was still snoring in the next room. Charles was upstairs making the bed. She must have imagined it, she thought. Slightly on edge now, but still tired, she decided to close her eyes once again. As she did so, she thought that she saw a dark hooded shape standing in the corner of the room, beside the long dark curtains. But her eyes were too heavy now to open again, and were fully closed by the time the figure moved closer.

***

"What are you doing?" Charles hissed, snatching away his hunched brother from the sleeping Jenna. His head had been so close to her face, his tongue tentatively reaching towards her cheek.

"He'll have her to himself soon enough, I just wanted a taste."

"If she's to be subjected to what Grandfather wants then that's Hell enough, without suffering the insult of your touch to begin with!" The anger was clear in Charles' tone despite how low he kept his voice.

"You never have been very respectful of your family, Charles. Happy to enjoy the wealth, the ease of life, the freedom from disease and slowness of age. But never happy to pay the prices that come along with it."

"I've never made any secret of my distaste for it."

"You're lucky you take after your mother and can go about the business of bringing the wives." Hugo pointed his bulbous forefinger in Charles' direction accusingly. "If I were able then Grandfather would have severed you from the bloodline long ago."

"That's right, you need me, don't you? And why is that, brother?"

Charles grabbed hold of his smaller, deformed sibling by the back of the neck and dragged him over to the window. It was dark outside now, and their reflection could be seen clearly staring back at them. Charles tore down the black hood that covered his brother's head, and let his brother look upon himself. The white, bulbous shape that stared in the black window was barely human. One eye was large, yellowed like a fish, the other a squinting pinprick of darkness. Purple veins throbbing against the skin, large growths covering the back of the hairless skull.

"I've more of him in me than you, brother." Hugo snarled, pulling his hood back up. "I'm more of the family than you."

"And that's exactly why you need me. Don't you forget it."

"You miss the clarity of your own point, brother. Our blood has been crossed too much now. Too many mothers and fathers both carrying our family strength. That's exactly why Grandfather wants to start a new line, so we can go abroad in the world as we once did."

"I've told you I'll do it. Now get out."

Jenna awoke not long after to see Charles standing in the corner of the room staring out of the window. She couldn't tell in the darkness, but was sure he was staring at the old tree.

"Are you alright?" she asked, seeing the tension in his shoulders.

"Just watching the storm." He replied without turning around. "If it blows that bloody tree down it will save you some work."

"I'll still charge you." She joked.

"I'd pay it." He replied, glancing back over his shoulder with a smile. "You know, that tree has been standing here longer than the house has. Our family blood is in it, you might say."

"Then why so keen to be rid of it?"

"You don't know my family. They want to keep things going, even though they've long since gone rotten."

"Families can be the best, can't they?" Jenna replied, her voice heavy with sarcasm. "Never asked this of a gay guy before, but would you mind taking me to bed?"

"First time for everything." Charles laughed, and then went over to help her.

***

"I almost feel I should be reading you a bedtime story." Charles joked as he stood beside Jenna, who had now settled into the large four poster bed that Charles had prepared for her.

"You can if you like. I rarely have company when I go to sleep these days, it'd be nice to talk whilst I drift off."

"Of course. I'm not sure I know any stories though."

"Do you know about the dragon?"

"Dragon?"

"Yeah, my dad once told me about this area. Said there was a local legend about a dragon or something that the villagers killed. Or made friends with. He said the ending wasn't clear."

"Ah, you mean the Wyrm. Not quite a dragon, but still an ancient creature that doesn't quite conform to modern day science."

"Ok so tell me about the Wyrm then." Jenna smiled, getting herself comfortable in the bed.

"Do I need to start with 'once upon a time'?" Charles joked.

"That's for fairy tales. Isn't this meant to be a true story?"

"It's a local legend, whether you'd call that a true story is another question." Charles laughed. "Anyway, long, long ago...and don't ask me when because I have no idea. Before the time of the Roman invasion, I believe...the people that settled on these lands made a startling discovery. A creature lived here, under the earth. A giant, ancient creature from a time before mankind. This creature, this Wyrm, could affect the weather, the ground itself, causing earthquakes or storms at will. The people of the settlement sent their bravest knight to fight it, and this is where the story diverts."

"It has multiple endings, right? Like most local legends."

"Exactly. The standard one is that the knight cut the creature's head off and that was the end of it. There are other endings, though, that say the Knight instead made a deal with the creature. In return for sparing it, the creature would give the Knight's family perfect weather and soil for crops, letting them grow rich. At the same time giving the reverse to rival settlements, eliminating competition."

"Monsters making business deals, I like it."

"I never said it was a monster." Charles said with a slight frown. "Just a creature nobody had seen before, or since. Like those green-hued monkeys they found in Brazil last year."

"Well I didn't mean any offence, if the Wyrm's listening." Jenna smirked. "Which version do you believe?"

"I was always partial to the third version. Where the Knight steadfastly refused the offer, but another settler saw sense, killed the knight, and took the offer themselves."

"Opportunistic, I like it."

"Well, I hope that sufficed as a bedtime story, Miss Reid. I don't have any others I'm afraid," said Charles, handing Jenna another glass of sparkling water. "There's more painkillers in that, it should help you sleep. And then we'll see about getting an ambulance in the morning. If we can't, then I'll get you there by car even if I have to drive over fields and through the middle of the wood."

"Are you sure you weren't the knight in that story?"

Charles smiled and gently brushed some hair from Jenna's face, then left the room and switched off the lights. His footsteps echoed in the long hallway, and he was close to the top of the staircase when he realised there were a second set of footfalls besides his own.

"I don't recall inviting you into the house, Hugo." Said Charles, turning to face his brother.

"Such a sweet little story you told her. Not the local history, I mean the one about taking her to the hospital. A comforting fairy tale. I do hope you don't believe it to be true?"

"I know that Grandfather wouldn't allow it, I'm not an idiot, brother. Now why are you in the house?"

"Just waiting for those 'pain killers' you gave her to take effect. Then we can move her to Grandfather's room."

"Tonight?"

"He's hungry. I assume those were sedatives you gave to her?"

"Of course they were, but only to help her sleep. Not as strong as the usual ones."

"Then she'll be awake for some of it." Hugo laughed. "And you thought you were being nice."

"Let me give her something stronger. For God's sake, Hugo, she doesn't have to endure it this way."

"I disagree, Grandfather likes it when they squirm." Hugo rasped with a low chuckle.

"You disgust me."

"Be that as it may, our blood is the same. And we have our duty. Once she's sound asleep, get her ready and bring her down to us. Grandfather can't wait to meet her."

"I'll take care of it." Charles sighed.

"Put her in the blue nightdress, he likes the blue one best."

"Just get out, Hugo!"

The black cloaked figure slinked away down the corridor, his cracked and breathless laughter filling the halls as he went.

***

Jenna awoke in the large bed, still-half asleep. She wasn't entirely sure what had awoken her, but something had cut through strange and disturbing dreams to bring her back here. Glancing around as best she could without risking too much movement, she scanned the darkness of the room. The branches of the old tree cast shadows on the wall that moved eerily in the breeze, the stuff of every horror film Jenna had ever watched. She smirked to herself, but then the smile disappeared from her face as quickly as it had appeared. Some of the shadows weren't shadows at all, but stretching, probing tendrils of greyish matter spreading across the walls and ceiling. She watched in horror as one of them wrapped itself around the upper frame of the bed posts, and then travelled down like a snake moving down a tree. Jenna screamed and a cold, bulbous hand covered her mouth.

"Shhh, he doesn't like noise, our Grandfather. He's used to the quiet, all the day down there." Said the monstrous humanoid form that had grabbed her. "Now let's get you ready for him."

Jenna bit into the hand that covered her mouth and tried to pull away from the arm that held her tight. Something cracked and popped in her side, reminding her instantly of the reason she was in this bed to begin with. The pain was so fierce that her eyes rolled up into her head and she was gone. When she next woke, Jenna was no longer in the bedroom.

"I'm sorry about this, I truly am." Came Charles' voice to her right. She was upright, sitting in a chair, but moving. It was dark, she couldn't quite tell where she was yet. The voice carried on. "I really did consider getting you to safety before all this happened, but there was no time. Grandfather is not easy to say no to, I'm afraid."

Jenna tried to cry out, but her mouth was tightly gagged, the material wrapped around the back of her head and biting tightly into her cheeks. Looking down she saw that she was bound by the wrists and ankles to an old wooden wheelchair, her clothes removed and instead replaced with an old blue nightdress. It was torn in places and stained with blood that wasn't hers. In a cold instant Jenna knew that she was not the first person to wear this. Frantically looking left and right, her eyes adjusted to the darkness and she realised that she was in a cave, or tunnel of some sort. The ground was damp, the sound of the wheels pressing against it gave that away as she was pushed forwards. Charles was on her right, so it wasn't him pushing the chair.

"Almost time for the wedding night." A voice behind her rasped, laughing wickedly.

"Shut up, Hugo." Charles snapped. "I feel I owe you an explanation, of sorts, Miss Reid. It's the least I can do. That story I told you earlier, it was true, in a manner of speaking. Except the bargain didn't end there. The Wyrm did everything it promised, but wanted a little more. The family it had made rich would become its own family. Women would be brought to it and impregnated with its seed. They would go out into the world, rich and prosperous, and carry a small piece of the Wyrm with them. Through them it would experience a world that was otherwise denied to it. You see the connection with its young was symbiotic, it felt what they felt and saw what they saw. But that works both ways, and it started to take on some human qualities."

Jenna struggled against her bonds to no avail, looking up at Charles pleadingly. He ignored her gaze, not able to meet it, and went on:

"Pride was one of them, of course, and hubris. Around the time of the Tudors, the Wyrm got into its head the idea of nobility, purity of blood and all that business. So, it began to, how would you say, 'keep it in the family'. Offspring bred with other offspring, as was his will. But that of course meant that there was a little more of him in each generation. And it started to show."

As he said this, Charles glanced at Hugo, pushing Jenna's wheelchair down the seemingly endless tunnel. Hugo glanced at his brother and frowned. Charles continued:

"Eventually, with so few children able to move comfortably in the world for him, the Wyrm changed his mind. New bloodlines were needed, which of course needed new women. He took to making his family bring them to him. Waifs and strays, as you'd expect. Those who wouldn't be missed. But sadly, they were never strong enough to withstand the impregnation, so new children were never born. And then you came along. For what it's worth, I am very sorry your employer didn't choose to send a male tree surgeon."

The tunnel opened up into an enormous subterranean cave, and Jenna found herself staring at a sight which was the stuff of nightmares. The roots of the tree she had been working on stretched down from the ceiling, except she saw now that it wasn't a tree, so much as a growth of some sort. And the thing it grew from lay on the floor in the centre of the cave. Easily forty feet long and perhaps half as wide, was a vast sickly white maggot-thing, a gaping black open maw at the front like a basking shark. From its body grew various tendrils, snaking out into the soil and the walls of the cave, with some forming stalactite-esque growths, the largest of which went above ground in the form of the old tree. Jenna screamed against her gag and struggled all the more, still to no avail. The pain in her side was throbbing, but it was barely a concern now.

"I suppose I should introduce Grandfather." Said Charles, gesturing towards the maggot. "You can probably guess his place in all this now, you're an intelligent woman. What I should add is that I really have no choice in this. I may be fortunate enough that it doesn't show, but Grandfather is inside me as he is all of my family. And if I disobey him, he can kill me with a thought. I don't want to die, who amongst us does? So here we are."

Jenna felt the wheelchair come to a stop, around fifteen feet away from the bulbous, pulsating monstrosity before her. The smell was like rotten eggs and foul meat, causing her to heave against her gag.

"Is she ready?" came another familiar voice from the shadows. It was Lincoln, except now he wasn't sat in a chair half covered by a blanket. Instead he was flopping towards them across the cave floor like a seal, his lower half revealed as being a white fleshy mass like the tail of any other maggot. Jenna screamed again, tears streaming down her face.

"Yes, I think so," Charles replied, then turned his attention back to Jenna. "For whatever small comfort it may be, the gestation period isn't overly long. You'll know in a matter of hours if the insemination was successful, and so will Grandfather. He can feel them growing inside of you, you see. Now, I don't know if prayer is of value to you, but I will offer you this one; Pray you die after the first litter. Because if it goes well, he'll just keep using you over and over until there's no more children to be born from you. Again, I am so deeply, deeply sorry for this."

"Come along nephew, let's leave Grandfather to his wedding night," said Lincoln, flopping along the floor past where Jenna sat immobile.

Charles placed a reassuring hand on Jenna's shoulder before he left, which she now recoiled at. Hugo could be heard laughing once more before he too left the cave, leaving Jenna alone with the Wyrm. As she watched in horror, several smaller tendrils grew from the mass of the thing, round lumps forcing their way to the surface and opening like popped bubbles revealing sickly yellow eyes underneath. Thousands of them now stared at her, as one more tendril made its way across the floor like an albino caterpillar. Jenna screamed and screamed as it slinked up her leg, the feeling against her flesh akin to standing in a pile of rotten wet leaves. Her eyes fixed on the end of the tendril just before it disappeared up beneath the hem of the blue nightdress, and watched as it grew fatter, thick and pulsing, and unmistakably phallic.

"Wonder if we'll have any girls. Been a while since we've had girls in the family." Hugo remarked as he and his kin left the tunnels, the sound of Jenna's unholy screams echoing deep in the earth behind them.

***

Just before dawn of that same night, Charles sat before the lit fireplace with his fifth glass of brandy. His constitution was strong, Grandfather's blood would do that for you, but even he was starting to feel a little drunk now. His guilt over the Reid girl had led to the bottle being opened, and it hadn't yet alleviated enough that he had decided to stop. Beside him on the floor was a pile of clothes and belongings that Jenna had left. Her van would be swallowed up by the earth, Grandfather would see to that, the rest was good for the fire. Charles reached down for the handbag and rifled through it idly. Phone, hairbrush, a pack of half eaten mints, and an envelope. Opened. Charles tossed the bag into the fireplace but kept hold of the envelope, noting the NHS logo in the top corner. Taking the contents out and unfolding it, his drunken eyes scanned the letter. Certain key words jumped out at him, the story being told simply that Jenna had indeed wanted to be a mother, but her body had decided otherwise. It was impossible for her to conceive.

Charles laughed to himself and downed the rest of his glass, then sat back in his chair. Not long afterwards the entire house started to shake, backed by the sound of an anguished and inhuman roar. The walls started to crack, plaster fell from the ceiling and the floorboards started to rupture. Charles's heart exploded in his chest as the walls of the Bullingdon family home came crashing down around him.

The End

Death, She Said

By

Edward Lee

"Life," I said.

I'd said it to myself, to my reflection in the rearview as I peeled the cardboard cover off the razor blade. Yeah, life.

I was all set; I was going to kill myself. Oh, I know what you're thinking. Sure, fella. All the time you're hearing about how suicidal tendencies are really just pleas for attention, cries for help. Fuck that. I didn't want help. I wanted to die.

I had one of those Red Devil brand blades, the kind you cut carpet with, or scrape paint off windows. Real sharp. I'd read somewhere that if you do it laterally, you bleed to death before the blood can clot. I sure as shit didn't want to pull a stunt like that and blow it. I could picture myself sitting in some psyche ward with bandaged wrists--a perfect ass. I wanted to do it right.

Why? Long story. I'll give you the abridged version.

I'd spent my whole life trying to make something good for myself, or maybe I should say what I *thought* was good turned out to be nothing. It was all gone in less time than it takes you to blow your nose. We had two kids. One ran off with some holistic cult, haven't seen him in a decade. The younger one died a couple weeks after her senior prom. "Axial metastatic mass," the neurologist called it. A fuckin' brain tumor is what I called it. Worst part was I never really knew them. It was my wife who brought them up, carried the load. I was too busy putting in 12, 14 hours a day at the firm, like airline trademark infringements were more important than raising my own kids. But I still had my wife, her love, her faith in me. She was behind me every step of the way, a real gem. She quit college to wait tables so I could go to law school, gave away her own future for me. She was always there--you know what I mean? We were going to get the house painted. She went out one day to check out some colors--I was too busy suing some company that made bearings for airplane wheels--but she never made it home. Drunk driver. I still had my job, though, right? Wrong. Month ago I was a senior partner in the number three firm in the country. A couple of associates decided it might be neat to bribe some jurors on a big air-wreck case I was litigating. They get disbarred, but I get blackballed. Right now, I couldn't get a job jacking fries at Burger Fucking King, my name stinks so bad. So I guess that wraps it up nice and neat. I'm a 48-year-old attorney with no job, no family, no life.

There.

I didn't want anyone saving me, calling the paramedics or anything like that. I decided I'd do it in my car. The repo people were already after it, so I figured let 'em have it with my blood all over the suede-leather seats. I backed into an alley off the porn block. Rats, oblivious to the cold, were hopping in and out of garbage cans. Lights from an adult bookstore blinked in my face. Up ahead, I could see the hookers traipsing back and forth on L Street. They were like the rats; they didn't feel the cold. You should've seen some of the wild shit they were wearing. Leopard-skin leotards, sheer low-cut evening dresses, shorts that looked like tin foil. It was kind of funny, that my last vision in life would be this prancing tribe of whores. I had the razorblade between my fingers, poised. Each time I got ready to drag it from the inside of my elbow to my wrist, I kept looking up. I wasn't chickening out, I just felt distracted. But distracted by what?

That's when I saw her, in that last half-moment before I was going to actually do it.

She'd probably been standing on the corner the whole time, I just hadn't noticed. It was like she was part of the wall, or even part of the city--darkness blended into brick.

She was staring right at me.

I stared back. She stood tall in a shiny black waistcoat whose hem came up to mid-thigh. Long legs, black stockings, high heels, I sensed she wasn't young--like the streetwalkers--yet she seemed more comely than old: graceful, beautiful in wisdom. Somehow I knew she couldn't be a hooker; looking at her, I thought of vanquished regalities--an exiled queen. She had her hands in her pockets, and she was staring.

Go away, I thought. *Can't you see I'm trying to kill myself?*

I blinked.

Then she was walking toward the car.

I stashed the razor blade under the seat. It didn't make sense. Even if she was a prostitute, no prostitute would approach a barely visible car in an alley. Maybe she'd think I was a cop. I could give her the brush-off and get back to business.

Her high heels ticked down the alley. Was she smiling? I couldn't tell. The rats scurried away.

She stopped beside the driver's window.

"I'm not sportin', I'm not datin', and I'm not looking for someone to tickle my stick," I said. "Buzz off."

Her voice was weird, like a wisp of breeze, or two pieces of silk brushing together. So soft it almost wasn't there. "Providence is a mysterious thing," she said. "It can be very nourishing."

I squinted. She was standing right there, but I couldn't see her, not really. Just snatches of her, like my eyes were a movie camera and the cameraman was drunk. All I could say in response was, "What?"

"Think before you act," she said. "There are truths you haven't seen. Wouldn't it be regrettable to die without ever knowing what they are?"

She couldn't possibly have seen what I was trying to do in the car; it was too dark, and she'd been too far away. Besides, the razor blade was under the seat.

"I can show you providence," she said. "I can show you truth."

"Oh, yeah?" I challenged. "What the fuck do you know about truth?"

"More than you think," she said.

I looked at her, still only able to see her in pieces, like slivers. I sensed more than saw. I sensed beauty in her age, not haggardness. I sensed gracility, wisdom . . .

"Come with me," she bid. "I'll show you."

I got out. *What the hell,* I thought. The razor would still be there when I got back. In my gut, though, it was more than that. In my gut, I felt *destined* to get out of the car.

She walked away.

I had to nearly trot to keep up. I could imagine how I must look to the people on the street: an unshaven, shambling dolt in a crushed $800 suit, hectically pursuing this...woman. Her high heels ticked across the cement like nails. The shiny waistcoat glittered. She took me back through the alley. Ahead, windows were lit.

"Look," she said.

Crack vials and glass crunched beneath my feet. Rotting garbage lay heaped against vomit- and urine-streaked brick.

I looked in the window, expecting to see something terrible. What I saw instead was this: A subsidized apartment, sparse but clean. Two black children, a boy and a girl, sat at a table reading schoolbooks, while an aproned woman prepared dinner in the background. Then a black man walked in, a jacket over his shoulder, a lunchpail in hand.

Beaming, the children glanced up. The woman smiled. The man kissed his wife, then knelt to hug his children.

But this wasn't terrible, it was wonderful. Jammed in a ghetto, surrounded by crime and despair, here was a family *making* it. Most didn't in this environment. Most fell apart against the odds. I was standing on crack vials and puke, looking straight into the face of something more powerful than any force on earth...

"Love," said the old woman.

Yeah, I thought. Love. I'm a lawyer, which means I'm also a nihilistic prick. You've heard the joke: What happens when a lawyer takes Viagra? He gets taller. But this made me feel good to see, the power of real love, real human ideals.

But why had the woman shown me this?

She was walking away again, and again I was huffing to keep up. Now I was curious--about her.

Where did she come from? What was her name? She led me through more grimy alleys, more garbage and havens for rats. A single sodium lamp sidelighted her. My breath condensed in the cold.

I tried to look at her...

All I could see was one side of her face from behind. Fine lines etched her cheek and neck. Her short, straight hair was dusted with gray. Yeah, she was up there-- 60ish, I guessed--but elegant. You know how some women keep their looks in spite of age--that was her. Well-postured, a good figure and bosom, nice legs. But I still never really got a look at her face.

In the next alley, muttering rose.

It was getting colder. I was shivering, yet the woman seemed comfortable, she seemed warm in some arcane knowledge. She pointed down.

Aw, shit, I thought. Strewn across the alley were bundles. They were people, the inevitable detritus of any big city. They lay asleep or unconscious: shivering dark forms wrapped in newspapers or rags. Many slept convulsing from the cold. The city was too busy repaving commuter routes to build more shelters. It was astonishing that on a night this cold they didn't just freeze to death. And all this time I thought I had nothing. Jesus.

"I don't want to see this," I said.

"Wait."

I heard footsteps. Then a bent shape was moving down the dark, stepping quietly between the twitching forms. It was a priest, an old guy, 70 at least. Slung across his back were blankets. I don't know how a guy his age could manage carrying all of them, especially in cold this bad. The guy huffed and puffed, stooping to cover each prone figure with a blanket. It was the look on his face that got to me most. Not pity, not fanaticism, just some kind of resolute complacency, like he was thinking. *Well, tonight I'll get whatever money I can lay my hands on, buy some blankets, and cover up some homeless people. No one else is gonna do it, so I'm gonna do it.* It was simple. Right now your average person was watching the reality shows, or getting laid, or sleeping in a warm bed, but here was this old priest doing what he could, for a few people no one else gave a pinch of shit about.

"Compassion," the woman, my companion, said.

I watched as the priest went about his business, shivering himself as he lay a blanket over each figure, one after another after another. Then I touched the woman's shoulder. "What is this?" I asked. "Why are you showing me this stuff? I don't get it."

"Providence," she whispered. "Come on."

Providence, I thought. She led. I followed. Now we were walking down Connecticut Avenue, the power drag. Lots of ritzy schmucks getting out of

132

limos in front of restaurants, where dinner for two cost more than the average working person made in two weeks. There were a lot of lawyers too, tisk, tisk. Whatever this tour was that she was taking me on--it was making me think.

Next we were walking past Washington Square, where I used to work, and 21 Federal, where I stopped for cocktails every day, or had power lunches with the managing partners. Jesus. A couple of blocks away people were sleeping in the fucking street, and we were too busy to care. Too busy hiding behind Harvard law degrees and clients who paid seven figures per annum just in retainers. This bizarre woman was showing me what I used to be. And she showed me this: I may have been a good attorney, but that sure as shit didn't mean I was a good person. An hour ago I was going to kill myself. Now all I could feel was shame. I felt like a spoiled baby.

"One more stop," she said. "Then you can go."

With the less I understood, the more I wanted to know. But one thing I *did* know: There was a reason for this. This was no ordinary encounter, and she was certainly no ordinary woman.

I half trotted along, always just behind her, never quite keeping up. It reminded me of the Dickens story, the wretched cynic shown his future and past by ghosts. But the woman was no ghost. I'd touched her; she was flesh.

She was real.

Minutes later we were standing in a graveyard.

Yeah, this was like the Dickens story, all right. My breath froze in front of my face. The woman stood straight as a chess piece, pointing down at the stone. But I already knew it wasn't *my* grave.

It was my wife's.

"Truth," the woman said.

Thoughts seemed to tick in my head; my

confusion felt like a fever.   First love, then compassion, and now...truth?

What truth was there in showing me my wife's grave? She'd been dead for years.

"Does it nourish you?" the woman asked. "The truth?"

Dead for years, yeah, but even in death she was the only real truth in my life.

"I loved her," I muttered.

"Indeed. And did she love you?"

"Yes."

"Yes?"

"Yes."

She paused, gauging me, I guess. "There, then," she told me. "There's truth even in memory. You should remember her love for you--the truth of it. It raises us up, doesn't it? It *nourishes* us." Her gaze seemed to wander. "The truth."

I wanted to cry. Now this final vision made sense. I'd had love. My wife had loved me. Lots of people, most people probably, never had love, not really. Just sad facsimiles and bitter falsehoods. I wanted to fall to my knees at this old woman's feet and blubber like a little kid. Because it wasn't cruelty that made her bring me here. It was the same force behind all the things she'd shown me tonight. Things to make me think and to see. Things to make me realize that life really was a gift, and that even when people died, even when the shittiest, most fucked up things happened, the gift remained...

We followed back the way we came, back through the bowels of the city. It was different now-- everything was. The streetlights made the pavement look gritty with ice. It began to snow but all I could feel was the warmth of what she'd shown me.

That's how I felt. I felt warm. I felt nourished.

She took me back to the alley, to the car. We got in. She sat beside me in the passenger seat.

"Time means nothing," she said. Her voice was soft, sweet in its age. "It never has."

"Who are you?" I asked.

She didn't answer. Instead she smiled, or at least she seemed to, because I still really couldn't see her. Just fragments of her, just shards of vision that never quite came together.

"You're some kind of angel, aren't you?" I finally summoned the nerve to ask. "You were sent to keep me from killing myself."

"Love, compassion, truth," she replied. "They add up to something. What a waste for a person to die alone, unnourished of the truth."

Yeah, she was an angel or something. The first thing she'd said to me was something about providence.

Greed, selfishness, cynicism, and God knows what else, had brought me to the brink of suicide but I'd been saved at the last minute by seeing the good things out there, the things that transcended the bad, the evil.

"The truth," she said.

"Thank you."

Somehow it didn't surprise me. She slipped out of the black waistcoat. She was nude beneath. Her breasts were large, with large full nipples. They sagged but gracefully. The gentle roll of flesh at her waist, the fine white skin of her throat, shoulders, and thighs, her entire body--seemed softly radiant in its age, beautiful in its truth.

That's what this was about--truth. And I knew why she'd taken off the coat. She hadn't brought me all this way just to fuck me in a Porsche 911. All night long she'd given me things to see. That's why she was naked now, to let me, at last, see *her*.

And I wanted to. I wanted to see the body which carried so resplendent a spirit. The light from the streetlamp shined through the windshield. I could see her body now, but still not her face, and I guessed I never would. This seemed appropriate, though, you've got to admit.

The face of an angel shouldn't be something you can ever really see.

"We're all here for a reason," she said, leaning over to look at me. "And this is my reason. To show the truth, to make people see the truth."

I held her hand, ran my fingers up her arm. I slid over close and began to touch her breasts, smoothed my fingers across her abdomen, down her thighs, and over the thick plot of her pubic hair. She seemed to expect this, like it was some kind of calm precognition. It wasn't lust, it wasn't sexual at all. I just wanted to touch her.

I needed to know what an angel felt like.

Her skin, though it had lost some of its elasticity, was soft and smooth as a baby's. Cool. Palely clean. The groove of her pubis sheathed my finger in heat.

Then she asked: "Are you ready to see the rest?"

"There's more?"

She paused. I think she liked this a lot, lazing back in the plush seat, being touched. "I've shown you love, compassion, and truth. I've nourished you, haven't I?"

"Yes," I said, still touching.

Her cool fingers entwined in mine. "But I need nourishment too, through something else."

"What?"

"Death," she said.

I stared at her. My hand went limp.

"The truth is like people. Sometimes the real face is the one underneath. Look now at what you didn't see before--the *rest* of the truth. The *real* truth."

She leaned over and kissed me. I turned rigid. Her cool lips played over mine, her tongue delved. All the while my eyes felt sewn open. I couldn't close them. The kiss reached into me and *pulled*. Yes, the kiss. It forced me to stare whimpering into the wide-open black chasm that was her face.

The *real* truth.

First, the future: The family in the window. The man, unemployed now, and drunk, was steadily beating his wife's face into a bleeding mask. Then, the boy, older, was holding a woman down while four others took turns raping her. He crammed a handful of garbage into her mouth to keep her quiet. "Watch me bust this bitch's coconut," he said when they were finished. He split her head open with a brick while the others divvied up her money.

Meanwhile, blocks away, his sister spread her legs for the tenth stranger of the night, her arms, hands, and feet pocked by needlemarks, her blood teeming with herpes, hepatitis, AIDS.

Next, the present: The alley of the homeless. The priest was gone. A gang of faceless youths chuckled as they poured gasoline over the huddled forms, drenching the new blankets. Matches flared. The alley burst into flames, and the gang ran off, laughing. Human flesh sizzled in each cocoon of fire. Screams wheeled up into the frigid night.

And last, the past: First, brakes squealing, a collision of metal, and my wife's neck snapping like a wine stem as her head impacted the windshield. Then the vision reeled back an hour. A hotel room. A bed. Naked on hands and knees, my wife was busily fellating a young man who stood before her. He held her head and remarked, "Yeah, Duff, this is one class-A cock-suck. She's fucking me with her tonsils." "Best deep throat in town, just like I told ya," remarked another man who then promptly inserted his vaselined penis into her rectum. "Bet your hubby would shit if he could see this, huh?" Eventually he ejaculated into her bowel. "Here comes lunch," said the first man, whose semen launched into her mouth. My wife swallowed it, purring like a cat. Then she lay back on the bed. "Can you believe it? I told him I was going to the paint store to check out color schemes for the house." "When you gonna dump that limp shithead?" inquired the second man. She began masturbating them both. "Why should I?" she said. "A deal like this? Come on! He keeps me in jewelry, and you guys keep me in cock." Then the three of them burst into laughter.

The kiss broke. I seemed to fall away from it, a rappeller whose line had just been cut. I sat slack in the seat. The old woman was looking at me, but I could see she wasn't old at all. She looked like a teenager. The meal she'd made of my truth left her robust, vital, glowing in new youth. Her once-gray hair shined raven-black. The pale skin had tightened over young muscle and bone; the large white orbs of her breasts grew firm even as I watched. Their fresh nipples erected, pointing at me like wall studs.

I couldn't speak. I couldn't move.

Greedy new hands caressed me; her eyes shined. She kissed me some more, licked me, reveled in what I was to her. Her breath was hot in my drained face.

"Just a little more," she panted.

She was drooling. She reached under the seat. The Red Devil razor blade glinted in icy light. Then, very gently, she placed it in my hand.

***

At least it didn't hurt. It felt good. It felt

purging. Know what I mean? Can't see much now. Like lights going down in a theater. All I can see is the little girl. She's watching me. She's grinning, getting younger and growing more alive on the meat of providence, on the sweet, sweet high of truth.

The End

Forbidden Fruit

By

Calvin Demmer

Billions of lightbulbs, plugged into the nighttime sky, illuminated the land.

Todd Watson awoke from a power nap and wiped dots of sweat off his forehead. Summer nights in the veld offered no respite from the heat of the day. At least he had shaved his head before the trip, already aware of the humidity and warmth he would have to endure. He sat up, looked at the bottoms of his boots, and pulled out the ash-white thorns that had found home in his soles. Mouthing choice curse words at the sweat covering his body, he looked at his friend Dan Matthews. He had scolded Dan less than an hour ago for wanting to start a small fire. The agitation he'd felt at Dan's rookie stupidity, dissipated as he watched his friend eating cold sausages from a can.

"Where's Bongani?" Todd asked.

Dan looked up, swallowing the sausage in his mouth. "Doing a quick scout of the area."

Todd reached for his rifle and got to his feet. "Well, that's great. Money we're paying him, and he comes and goes as he pleases. Some guide he's turning out to be."

"Well, I think it's good. I wouldn't want to run into any dangerous animals if I didn't have to."

"This is Africa, Dan. Everything here is dangerous."

Todd sat next to his friend.

"Do you want what's left of the sausages?" Dan asked.

"No, thanks."

Dan pulled his sleeves down. His skin was noticeably fair, even at night. "So what culture is Bongani from?"

"Well, Zulu originally, but I'm not sure, to be honest. He's a bit of a rogue. He can speak many of the languages around here, and he's done all sorts of work all round Africa, which is what matters."

"Ah, okay."

Staring into the distance, Todd shook his right leg. It was never easy to calm the current that pulsated throughout his body when he was on a job, and this was deadly work after all. Poaching was a serious offense in Southern Africa. They wouldn't be the first to get into a firefight with the park rangers. On top of that, you never knew what wildlife you could run into.

"Did he say how long he'd be?" Todd asked.

"Nope."

The three of them had been dropped off near one of the national park's borders. On foot, they had entered through a weak spot in the fence. They then dashed deep into the park, where there would be less patrols than on the perimeter. They left all electronics behind, fearful any instruments could be used to locate them.

"Well, I guess we ought to be preparing for the night," Todd said. "These tents aren't going to put themselves up. Trust Bongani to miss all the work."

"He said to wait until he checked out the area."

"You got to be kidding me. Who is paying who here?"

Dan kept quiet.

"Come on now, up. Let's get this shit going. I'm not gonna wait until Bongani has finished dancing to some ancestor so he can sleep comfortably."

Dan stumbled after Todd.

"You all right there?" Todd asked, reaching into his large backpack.

"Yeah, the old right knee takes a few moments to warm up."

After an hour there was still no sign of Bongani. Todd and Dan had erected all the tents, checked their gear, and prepared a cold meal for Bongani's return. The two sat with legs outstretched as they gazed at the sky. They inhaled the dusty, dry atmosphere of the barren world around them.

"Where the hell is he?" Todd mumbled.

"Being thorough, I hope."

Todd chuckled. "Bongani is a pro. He'll be fine. I'm more worried he's gone and taken a snooze in a tree. Anyway, I told you this isn't like our excursions into Asia. You better have what it takes to do this."

"I—"

The patter of feet on the hard soil stopped Dan from defending the weight he had gained the last few months. Bongani appeared, running toward the two men. He came at such a speed that he didn't have time to slow down and toppled over one of the tents.

Bongani was back up in a flash. "We have to go now."

Todd frowned. "Why? We just got everything sorted."

"That does not matter. The rangers are coming." Bongani moved for his backpack and filled it with any items near him. He zipped it closed, lifted it onto his back, and started jogging.

Todd looked around, considering if he should try to pack one of the tents, but a low humming sound stopped him. The sound got louder.

"Fuck," Todd said. "Get your bag, Dan. We're going to have to run."

"And all the stuff?"

"That's a chopper coming." Todd grabbed his pack and ran after Bongani. Their guide moved fast with considerable ease.

Dan eventually caught up with them, but by then the chopper's blades sounded like a whirlpool in the sky.

Todd peered back and saw a spotlight shining down. More lights shone in the blackness behind them. "I count three vehicles with the chopper."

"We're fucked," Dan said. "Holy shit, we're fucked."

"Calm down, you fool. Bongani, what are our chances?"

"Better if we run faster." Bongani picked up the pace.

Todd lost track of time. He kept a steady pace as they pressed on, motivated by the lack of noise, especially the fading chopper. Even the shrubs that would wrap around his feet and the bigger stones tipping his balance, couldn't slow him down. He sensed the three of them were getting away from the rangers. Bongani seemed to agree and eventually slacked off the pace. Dan, wheezing a few feet behind Todd, was audibly thankful when they hit a jog.

Bongani stopped.

Todd took the moment to regulate his breathing and heard Dan panting; Bongani seemed fine. The stars in the sky provided decent illumination, but Todd wanted a better idea of where they were. He switched on the only flashlight they had taken during the escape and shined its beam around the area. There were some low-growing bushes close by and a few trees around them farther on.

"We shall rest here," Bongani said.

Dan plopped down on the ground. "Thank goodness."

"What you thinking, Bongani? Did we lose them?" Todd asked.

"Hard to say. Maybe."

"That all you gonna give me, mister expert?"

"We should rest. Tomorrow will be a long day."

Todd waved Bongani off and went to sit next to Dan. He hated the fact that they had lost so much gear, especially as he was the one who'd fronted the costs. His mind kept active as he lay on the hard soil and stared at the sky. He needed to find a way to salvage the operation.

"*Lala kahle,*" Bongani said in Zulu.

Todd ignored him. He didn't want to say good night back. If Bongani hadn't walked to scout the area, maybe the rangers wouldn't have found them.

* * *

Morning brought a clear cerulean sky. Todd swore at his jacket, which had been his makeshift bed. It had done nothing to soften the hard African ground. There was no breeze to caress his senses, and he continued his curses at the prospect of the forthcoming hot, dry day. Why did he do this kind of work? As he got older the gnawing guilt within grew stronger, as he knew this wasn't the work of a good person. He had a wife and young child. They needed him around and not in a jail cell somewhere. They also needed money, and this work was what Todd knew.

He tapped Dan on the shoulder. "Ten minutes."

Dan, with his arms wrapped over his head, didn't reply.

Todd stood, stretched, and wandered off to a heap of rocks about twenty yards from where they had slept. Bongani was using one of the flatter-shaped rocks as a seat. He gazed across the veld and spoke without turning around to face Todd.

"*Sawubona*, Mister Watson."

"Morning, Bongani."

"*Unjani?*"

"I've been better. How are you?"

"Same, but I am alive, and that means I can change my situation."

Todd shrugged. "Great, so let's get real. How bad is it? Are we fucked?"

"No. The land can provide, and the wrong animals we can avoid. It is the rangers we will have to be watchful for, especially as they likely will have found the gear. That may have been what gave us the time to escape, but it will also have sent them into red alert."

"But the wildlife? If we can't avoid them, that is, we have one rifle between us, not a lot of ammo, and one panga."

"Do not worry." Bongani tossed a stone into a bush a few feet from him. "The wrong animals I can keep us away from. I told you. As for what you really want to know but do not ask, my acquaintances and I have done the job before with much less."

Todd turned back to Dan. There was still no sign of movement. He spat on the dusty earth. "Good to hear, Bongani."

When Dan awoke, the men shared a bag of nuts and a tin of beans, then set off on the next part of their mission. Bongani was confident he knew where the rhinos liked to graze during the day. However, he had warned them it was an arduous journey. The previous night had seen them run in the wrong direction from their objective. Todd wasn't worried about the distance. His dilemma was the limited arsenal at their disposal, but he was desperate to come away with something. The once ten-day-long planned haul had turned into a three-day hit-and-run.

* * *

The walk was mundane. Apart from the occasional shift away from the odd pack of animals, which Bongani knew by checking for tracks, there wasn't much activity or any sightings of anything. The terrain also didn't offer much in terms of view. Todd grew tired of the same prickly bushes, loose stones, and sharp thorn trees. Bongani, however, had become more agitated as the day moved on, eventually mumbling to himself. Todd couldn't resist prying.

"Bongani, is something troubling you?"

Bongani stopped. He got onto his haunches, almost as if he were checking for tracks again, and moved some of the soil around. "Something is not right."

"What?"

"I am not sure, but I have heard stories of this."

"Stories of what?" Todd held his hands up.

"The landscape is not how it should be. And the smell, it is ashy, almost like the air after a fire. I fear we have entered an old realm. On one of my trips I heard a *sangoma* speak much of this."

"What's a *sangoma*?" Dan asked.

"They're traditional healers," Todd said. "But also, they're meant to be able to speak to spirits or gods, protect their people, and fight evil. If you believe that shit."

"It is not shit," Bongani said.

"Bongani, has the sun gotten to you? Great. Just what we need: our guide is going nuts from heatstroke."

"No, I am fine. This problem is real. I have not encountered it before, but I know we must keep on until we get back into our world."

Todd placed his hand on his forehead. "Yeah, yeah. Let's get back to our world before the aliens arrive."

"Try not to look around too much. If you see or hear anything odd, keep moving. You do not notice anything, and hopefully, nothing notices you."

Dan shook his head. "No, no, no. That's too creepy."

"Oh, please," Todd said. "The rangers, now, they're what we have to be worried about and not some mumbo jumbo of being lost in some old realm. Hell, what's next? Dinosaurs?"

Bongani stood. His temples strained as he walked ahead. "Do as I say, please, and we should be fine."

Todd labored forward. Bongani's strange tale couldn't prevent the trek from becoming monotonous again. The hot sun burned his face as his eyes grew tired. He jolted when Dan tapped his shoulder.

"What?"

"Check over there." Dan pointed to their left.

There was a strange little tree, all on its own, in the middle of nowhere. The tree was unlike any Todd had seen in the park with its large lush leaves, its thick chocolate-colored trunk, and the bright green grass growing around it.

"Come on, let's check it out," Todd said.

The two men jogged to the tree and found peculiar oval-shaped purple fruits hanging from its branches. They looked juicy and had a sweet aroma. The saliva ran in Todd's mouth; Dan picked one of the fruits.

"Aikona, aikona." Bongani ran to them. "No, no, no, we do not eat this."

Dan didn't release the fruit.

Bongani slapped it out of his hand. *"Hamba, hamba."*

"What the hell is it?" Todd asked. "Is it poisonous, Bongani?"

"No, but it is not of our time. We must leave this tree alone. I believe it is the source of seeing that which has passed. Very bad, very bad. You do not wish to see such things. You do not wish to invite such things to see you. Come now, you are wasting time. You do not listen. We must keep moving forward to get back to our time. Do you want to be stuck here forever? You never know when these realms open or close."

"Are the fruits some kind of hallucinogenic?"

"No, what you see is real. But you waste time with such questions. Come now, okay?"

163

Todd gave him a thumbs-up, faking agreement. Bongani had said it wasn't poisonous and it wasn't a hallucinogenic. That was good enough for him. As soon as Bongani walked ahead, he turned to Dan and indicated for him to snatch some of the fruits. Dan duly obliged and picked a few of the juiciest-looking ones, then hid them in his pack.

The two men caught up with Bongani, who had increased the pace again. Todd felt a slight bit of concern regarding Bongani, as the heat could do strange things to a person. His story of an old realm and then the reaction to the tree didn't sit right.

Todd was glad he carried the rifle.

* * *

They were covering decent ground when Todd became annoyed by the stiffness in his neck. He massaged the lower right side and looked up. At first, he assumed there was something wrong with his eyesight as the sky appeared to have a light purple shimmer. He blinked and focused. The strange color remained.

"The sky is..." Dan said.

"Purple," Todd added. "Probably some phenomenon, like—"

"Huh," Bongani interrupted. "No phenomenon I know of. This is old times. We are still not in our time."

Todd looked at Dan, shaking his head.

The sky did change color again, this time to a light gray. Dusk had fallen. They'd been walking the entire day and had found no food or water. With their supplies at a critical low, this was fast becoming a serious problem.

Bongani stopped.

"What's it now?" Todd asked.

"Shhh." Bongani placed his index finger over his mouth.

Dull *thud*s echoed when all was still. They weren't random; they had a pattern. One dull *thud* came, and then two quicker *thud*s. It could be animals on the march? Todd quickly ceased the idea as nonsense. The sound was too rhythmic. It had a beat.

"Drums?" Dan asked.

Bongani nodded. "Come, come. We must move away quick."

"But who the hell would be playing drums out here?" Todd asked.

He got no reply. Bongani jogged at a quick pace. Infuriated, Todd bolted after him. He was about to physically push on their guide when he saw the landscape ahead was changing. There were trees and bushes that he recalled belonging in this part of Africa. To his left, he even thought he saw two giraffes in the distance, but with night almost upon them, he wasn't sure.

Bongani stopped again, got to his knees, and picked up some of the soil. Slowly, he let it fall from his hand. He took off his backpack and dropped it next to him. It wasn't quite a smile, but a brief grin appeared over his face. Todd noted it was the first time Bongani looked relaxed since mentioning the old realm.

"We have made it," Bongani said. "We are back in our time."

"Great." Todd decided not to ask Bongani who could make drum sounds out here. He assumed the sounds were yet another phenomenon of the wild, but he had to admit on some level it was a bit odd. He had been to different parts of Africa on many occasions, but this was the first time he'd seen purple skies shimmering overhead or heard drums in the middle of a protected animal park.

"We will have to camp here tonight. We will only get to the rhino tomorrow, thanks to the old realm wasting our time."

"Sounds like a plan, I guess." Todd frowned. How good of a guide was Bongani, truly? He'd come highly recommended by some people who had ventured into the country on "special" trips. Yet Todd couldn't shake the idea that he had spun the tale of the old realm to cover for not knowing his way around, which led them to spend an entire day searching for the rhinos. Secondly, they hadn't come across water, and the only fruit they'd discovered had caused a strange reaction from Bongani.

Bongani patted his chest. "I shall keep first watch, and you two can get some rest. I will scout the area a bit first. Do not worry."

"You want some food before you go?" Dan asked. "We still got an energy bar or two and some snacks."

"No, not now. You two eat and rest."

Bongani headed out into landscape held firmly in the grip of night.

Todd and Dan ate an energy bar and drank some water. With no tents or sleeping bags, they had to try and find spots on the ground that were level and as soft as possible. Only conversation and the stars above were their entertainment. Their chat didn't last long, as both men were tired from the long day. The stars held their gazes as eyelids became heavy.

The roar of an engine startled Todd. The sound was impressive in the still night air, and he sprang up, ready for action. It was too dark to see what was coming their way. He grabbed the rifle; Dan, also up, took the panga. They huddled behind a nearby bush.

Bongani shouted in the distance.

As he neared, Todd could make out his distant silhouette. "If that fool has brought the rangers to us again, I swear I'm shooting him."

"What's he saying?" Dan asked.

"Fuck knows, but I hear the engine coming closer."

"Wait, I think he said Jimmy or get-gym-ga."

"*Gijima*?"

"Yeah, that's it. What's it mean?"

"Run."

A gunshot, close by, invaded the night. Both men grabbed what they could and ran. Todd turned his neck to glance at what unfolded behind them. Bongani appeared to stand still, but then he dropped to the ground. Bright floodlights on a vehicle switched on and illuminated the spot where their guide had fallen.

"What happened?" Dan asked.

"Don't look. Keep running."

"Where are we going?"

"Not sure. I think it's the way we came."

"What are we going to do?"

"Just fucking run."

"We're running away from the rhino again."

"Dan, you idiot. They shot Bongani."

* * *

There was no escape from the heat as both men ran into the night. Perspiration poured down their faces as their pace slowed due to exhaustion. They found the bushes and loose rocks underfoot more treacherous, and both had fallen once or twice during their getaway. It was harder without a guide ahead of them. Why did the rangers have to shoot

Bongani? Sure, his skills appeared to be all over the place as a guide, but he had been a good person at heart. He could've learned and improved. Todd resisted any more sadness with ease, as he had done many times before.

He shined his flashlight every now and again and noticed that the wildlife and plant life waned once more. This time there were no drums and the sky didn't change color. Todd assumed they would find the clearing that Bongani had called the center of the old realm. He didn't believe in such myths and legends, but he didn't like the idea of being too out in the open. It took away any shelter or cover but could aid the speed of their escape. He scanned his sides.

"Here," Todd said, shining his flashlight at some nearby bushes. "Let's stop here. We'll take a quick break. If we hear the rangers, we keep moving."

"I don't hear the vehicles anymore."

"Yeah."

"Poor Bongani. Why would they shoot him?"

Todd kicked at the ground beneath his feet. "Fuck knows, maybe he resisted arrest. Maybe he attacked one of them. All I know is I wouldn't want to be apprehended in this shithole."

Dan nodded, taking a seat on the ground.

"What we got to eat?" Todd asked.

Dan searched through his bag. "A protein bar, a can of beans, and a bag of nuts—oh, and four of those strange fruits."

"Fuck it, let's try one of them."

Todd ripped open one of the peculiar fruits. It didn't smell off, nor did it smell like peaches or almonds, which was a good sign. He placed some of the juice on his finger; he saw and felt no irritation. Todd put some of the juice on his lips. It didn't burn.

The taste was sweet, so sweet he couldn't resist licking his lips.

"Good enough for me." Todd took a bite.

Both men ate. The fruit burst with flavor. It was exactly what they required, and energy surged through Todd's body. The world around him seemed brighter, clearer.

"Damn, that was good," Dan said. "Seconds?"

"No, we should keep the other two in case we don't find anything for a while. It's safe to say this operation has been a bust. I'll have to worry about the lost cash when we get back. At least we won't have to pay Bongani his other half." Todd curled his hand into a fist. "What a wasteful expense he turned out to be. We need to get the fuck out of here."

"Yeah…"

"We'll have to keep going back until we find a perimeter fence."

Dan stood, rocking from side to side.

"You all right?" Todd asked.

"Yeah, yeah. Just a bit groggy."

"Must be the heat."

They decided to press on through the night. The call of home and the boost from the fruit now fueled their muscles. After a while, Todd thought he could see the clearing they had passed earlier in the day. He loathed having to traverse it, but they had no other choice, so he carried on, only to feel Dan pull on him.

"What the hell, man?"

"Wow. Look over there. Don't you see them?"

Todd strained his eyes under the starry sky. He saw nothing but the emptiness of the clearing ahead. "What do you see?"

"There are animals everywhere."

"This isn't a time for jokes."

"I'm not joking. There are elephants, giraffes, zebras, gazelles, and so much more. But they look odd, a bit hazy, and they all have a blue shimmer." Dan stepped forward. "I want to see them closer."

Todd reached for his friend, who pulled free from the grip. "Wait, Dan. I think you're tripping. I feel fine, so it's not the fruit. Must be from the sun earlier. You need to take a breather and get some water."

Dan didn't listen. He upped his pace and jogged into the clearing, heading for its center.

Todd shook his head while keeping his distance from Dan, deciding to let his delusions play out—so long as he was quiet. There were no signs of lights anywhere around them. He could only hope the rangers had quit for the night.

"Rhinos," Dan said. "Todd, there are rhinos here, and they're everywhere."

"Okay, Dan. Take it easy now. You sure you don't want some water?"

"They're circling me, and one is coming forward."

"You're having a bad trip. Relax." Todd decided enough was enough. He marched to Dan. His plan was to get his friend to sit and have some water.

Dan lifted off the ground, his body flying backward like a rag doll. At first, Todd thought he was hallucinating as well, but when Dan crashed back to the ground, the truth of their current situation hit him hard.

"What the fuck?" Todd ran to his friend's aid.

Dan was inert. Todd tried talking to him, but he got no reply. He shined the flashlight over his friend and saw the blood pooling all around him. Icy tendrils shot down his spine. He rolled Dan onto his back, gasping as he saw the massive hole in his chest. He checked Dan's vitals, and the truth surfaced.

He was dead.

Todd looked around, seeking someone or something to blame. He was confused, and his mind thundered as he tried to find a tether to reality, but he remained stuck, grasping at liquid thoughts. A large shadow moved in his peripheral vision. As he turned his head, a rhino-like shape disappeared into the darkness.

"Come back, you fuck."

Another form moved to his right. Todd turned in time to see a shape like the first headed for him. Before the impact, he glimpsed the animal. It was a rhino. The beast, adorned in a sparkling powder-blue coating, lowered its head and aimed its horn at him. The rhino vanished, but Todd sensed the impact was coming. His body lifted into the air as a magnificent force struck him.

Everything went dark when he hit the ground.

* * *

Todd awoke, rattled. He sat up, realizing he must have passed out. Fragmented images shot up in the fore of his mind. How many of them had been real? He figured the fruit must have been some hallucinogenic after all, and a warmth rose in his core. If it was all a bad trip, Dan was alive.

Footsteps approached from behind him.

"Dan?"

"No, I am not Dan," someone said.

Todd turned around. The short dark man before him wore a strange and colorful ensemble. A feather stuck out from some band on his head, there were colorful beads on his arms, and a type of animal-skin loincloth covered him. He held a walking stick with a large ball at its top. The man seemed calm as he stared at Todd.

"Who are you? What do you want? Where am I?" The questions shot out of Todd's mouth in quick-fire succession, surprising him.

"I am a *sangoma*. I wanted to communicate with a certain old one. You are in the old realm."

"What? What's going on? I want to get out of here. Where's Dan?"

"Dead one, you ask many questions. It is not necessary anymore. I do not know what you have done to anger the old ones, but there is nothing that can be done for you. As for your Dan, I fear he is dead. They may have allowed him to move on to a different realm to see out the times. You, they have not."

"Why do you keep calling me 'dead one'?"

The *sangoma* looked to the sky. "Do you see the sun?"

Todd looked to the heavens. "No, I don't. What the fuck? Where is it? Tell me now. What trickery is this?"

"For you, the sun is gone. You have died, and recently. Soon the blue skies you have known will also fade. You will wander these empty lands under the purple skies. It is best to accept it. I feel for you. It is not a nice way to spend eternity, away from others passed, even for one who has angered the old ones. Though, you will have many animals for company."

"I'm sick of this mumbo-jumbo bullshit. Fuck you and all your so-called old ones. I'm out of here."

"You will never be able to leave the sound of the drums. They are a protection we have put to stop anything coming through into our time. I am afraid that the drums are the border of your world now, dead one."

Todd waved off the *sangoma* and walked ahead. The anger rose within him as he tried to determine how much he truly loathed Africa. He turned around to launch some more choice words at the *sangoma*.

The man was gone.

Todd heard an oncoming vehicle. It was most likely the park rangers, but he had endured enough and decided to give himself up. As they approached, he put his hands over his head. Instead of driving toward him, the rangers stopped a couple hundred yards ahead. All three of the men in the vehicle got out. They searched the land.

"Hey, over here," Todd shouted.

No response came, and he jogged to them.

He heard them talking, but he couldn't make out what they said. The words sounded as if they were coming through a distorting old radio. He walked to one of the rangers and patted him on the back. His hand went through the man, and Todd found himself toppling forward onto the ground.

"What the fuck is going on?"

The men ignored him, and one of them picked up Todd's rifle.

Todd focused as hard as he could to try and understand what the men were saying. He heard broken parts here and there.

"...all three are dead..."

"...body was found over...vehicle now..."

"What the fuck are you talking about?" Todd made his way to the back of their vehicle, a dusty, well-used pickup. He investigated the back. There was a blanket over a concealed shape. The shape, Todd realized, was that of a body.

"Is it Dan? Bongani? You assholes, what have you done?"

Todd used all the might he could muster, which was barely enough to lift a side of the blanket off the corpse, or had a bit of wind helped? Either way, it sufficed. He could see the face. It didn't belong to either Dan or Bongani.

It was his.

He stood motionless as the men got into the pickup and drove off. Realizing he needed to do something, he ran after them. He screamed, swore, and begged for them to stop. Confusion enveloped him. Fear flooded within.

Todd ran into an invisible wall and toppled backward. The sounds of the drums came. At first, they were soft, but they continued to get louder. Todd's head threatened to explode. He kept retreating, eventually losing all track of time and distance. When the drums were a faint tapping sound, he stopped.

The sky had returned to the peculiar shade of purple. Looking around, Todd determined he was back in the center of the old realm's clearing. He saw the animals that Dan had seen. They all sparkled blue as they made their way over the landscape. Somehow, he knew every one of them was dead and that they were now ghosts of the past. They were living out eternity, grazing and wandering, as they had done their entire lives.

Todd looked at his hands.

They sparkled blue.

The End

Made in the USA
Middletown, DE
28 May 2022